Cargo of Coffins

SELECTED FICTION WORKS BY L. RON HUBBARD

FANTASY
The Case of the Friendly Corpse

Death's Deputy

Fear

The Ghoul

The Indigestible Triton

Slaves of Sleep & The Masters of Sleep

Typewriter in the Sky

The Ultimate Adventure

SCIENCE FICTION
Battlefield Earth

The Conquest of Space

The End Is Not Yet

Final Blackout

The Kilkenny Cats

The Kingslayer

The Mission Earth Dekalogy*

Ole Doc Methuselah

To the Stars

ADVENTURE
The Hell Job series

WESTERN
Buckskin Brigades

Empty Saddles

Guns of Mark Jardine

Hot Lead Payoff

A full list of L. Ron Hubbard's
novellas and short stories is provided at the back.

*Dekalogy—a group of ten volumes

L. RON HUBBARD

Cargo
of
Coffins

GALAXY
PRESS

Published by
Galaxy Press, LLC
7051 Hollywood Boulevard, Suite 200
Hollywood, CA 90028

Printed in the United States of America.

ISBN-10 1-59212-352-X
ISBN-13 978-1-59212-352-0

Library of Congress Control Number: 2007927535

Contents

Stories from Pulp Fiction's Golden Age

A ND it *was* a golden age. The 1930s and 1940s were a vibrant, seminal time for a gigantic audience of eager readers, probably the largest per capita audience of readers in American history. The magazine racks were chock-full of publications with ragged trims, garish cover art, cheap brown pulp paper, low cover prices—and the most excitement you could hold in your hands.

"Pulp" magazines, named for their rough-cut, pulpwood paper, were a vehicle for more amazing tales than Scheherazade could have told in a million and one nights. Set apart from higher-class "slick" magazines, printed on fancy glossy paper with quality artwork and superior production values, the pulps were for the "rest of us," adventure story after adventure story for people who liked to *read*. Pulp fiction authors were no-holds-barred entertainers—real storytellers. They were more interested in a thrilling plot twist, a horrific villain or a white-knuckle adventure than they were in lavish prose or convoluted metaphors.

The sheer volume of tales released during this wondrous golden age remains unmatched in any other period of literary history—hundreds of thousands of published stories in over nine hundred different magazines. Some titles lasted only an issue or two; many magazines succumbed to paper shortages during World War II, while others endured for decades yet. Pulp fiction remains as a treasure trove of stories you can read, stories you can love, stories you can remember. The stories were driven by plot and character, with grand heroes, terrible villains, beautiful damsels (often in distress), diabolical plots, amazing places, breathless romances. The readers wanted to be taken beyond the mundane, to live adventures far removed from their ordinary lives—and the pulps rarely failed to deliver.

In that regard, pulp fiction stands in the tradition of all memorable literature. For as history has shown, good stories are much more than fancy prose. William Shakespeare, Charles Dickens, Jules Verne, Alexandre Dumas—many of the greatest literary figures wrote their fiction for the readers, not simply literary colleagues and academic admirers. And writers for pulp magazines were no exception. These publications reached an audience that dwarfed the circulations of today's short story magazines. Issues of the pulps were scooped up and read by over thirty million avid readers each month.

Because pulp fiction writers were often paid no more than a cent a word, they had to become prolific or starve. They also had to write aggressively. As Richard Kyle, publisher and editor of *Argosy*, the first and most long-lived of the pulps, so pointedly explained: "The pulp magazine writers, the best of them, worked for markets that did not write for critics or attempt to satisfy timid advertisers. Not having to answer to anyone other than their readers, they wrote about human beings on the edges of the unknown, in those new lands the future would explore. They wrote for what we would become, not for what we had already been."

Some of the more lasting names that graced the pulps include H. P. Lovecraft, Edgar Rice Burroughs, Robert E. Howard, Max Brand, Louis L'Amour, Elmore Leonard, Dashiell Hammett, Raymond Chandler, Erle Stanley Gardner, John D. MacDonald, Ray Bradbury, Isaac Asimov, Robert Heinlein—and, of course, L. Ron Hubbard.

In a word, he was among the most prolific and popular writers of the era. He was also the most enduring—hence this series—and certainly among the most legendary. It all began only months after he first tried his hand at fiction, with L. Ron Hubbard tales appearing in *Thrilling Adventures*, *Argosy*, *Five-Novels Monthly*, *Detective Fiction Weekly*, *Top-Notch*, *Texas Ranger*, *War Birds*, *Western Stories*, even *Romantic Range*. He could write on any subject, in any genre, from jungle explorers to deep-sea divers, from G-men and gangsters, cowboys and flying aces to mountain climbers, hard-boiled detectives and spies. But he really began to shine when he turned his talent to science fiction and fantasy of which he authored nearly fifty novels or novelettes to forever change the shape of those genres.

Following in the tradition of such famed authors as Herman Melville, Mark Twain, Jack London and Ernest Hemingway, Ron Hubbard actually lived adventures that his own characters would have admired—as an ethnologist among primitive tribes, as prospector and engineer in hostile climes, as a captain of vessels on four oceans. He even wrote a series of articles for *Argosy*, called "Hell Job," in which he lived and told of the most dangerous professions a man could put his hand to.

Finally, and just for good measure, he was also an accomplished photographer, artist, filmmaker, musician and educator. But he was first and foremost a *writer*, and that's the L. Ron Hubbard we come to know through the pages of this volume.

This library of Stories from the Golden Age presents the best of L. Ron Hubbard's fiction from the heyday of storytelling, the Golden Age of the pulp magazines. In these eighty volumes, readers are treated to a full banquet of 153 stories, a kaleidoscope of tales representing every imaginable genre: science fiction, fantasy, western, mystery, thriller, horror, even romance—action of all kinds and in all places.

Because the pulps themselves were printed on such inexpensive paper with high acid content, issues were not meant to endure. As the years go by, the original issues of every pulp from *Argosy* through *Zeppelin Stories* continue crumbling into brittle, brown dust. This library preserves the L. Ron Hubbard tales from that era, presented with a distinctive look that brings back the nostalgic flavor of those times.

L. Ron Hubbard's Stories from the Golden Age has something for every taste, every reader. These tales will return you to a time when fiction was good clean entertainment and the most fun a kid could have on a rainy afternoon or the best thing an adult could enjoy after a long day at work. Pick up a volume, and remember what reading is supposed to be all about. Remember curling up with a *great story*.

—Kevin J. Anderson

KEVIN J. ANDERSON *is the author of more than ninety critically acclaimed works of speculative fiction, including The Saga of Seven Suns, the continuation of the Dune Chronicles with Brian Herbert, and his New York Times bestselling novelization of L. Ron Hubbard's Ai! Pedrito!*

Cargo of Coffins

CHAPTER ONE

When Enemies Meet

THE tattered giant saw Destiny standing against a blindingly white wall. But he did not recognize Paco Corvino as Destiny. Paco Corvino was the last man Lars Marlin had expected to see in Rio de Janeiro.

The first reaction was surprise but it quickly gave way to a surge of stolid hate which made Lars Marlin clutch the butt of the .38 inside his sun-bleached, wind-ripped shirt.

Paco Corvino deserved to die, had merited death for years, but now, as always, he stood in too obvious a position to be killed. Thinking of killing Paco was pleasant, and Lars stood where he was in the blue depths of a shadowy entrance considering it.

Across the street a dusky, booted policeman stood vigilantly under an awning. Lars saw him and drew back instinctively. Again the giant's chill gaze, bitter as an arctic sea, turned to all-unknowing Paco.

The butt of the .38 was sweaty in Marlin's palm. The temptation was great. Did the risk warrant the pleasure of revenge? One well-placed shot at this range of forty feet and Paco would drop off the curb and into the gutter. His confident, insinuating smile would be frozen forever upon his too-handsome face.

The butt of the .38 was sweaty in Marlin's palm.
The temptation was great. Did the risk
warrant the pleasure of revenge?

Lars drew the .38 up a little, still keeping it out of sight. How he had prayed for this chance! For years without end he had waited patiently to even up a long-standing score.

But with the mud of the swamps of French Guiana hardly dry upon his bare feet, Lars was running a double risk. Any suspicious move from him would bring investigation from the Rio police, and that investigation would send Lars Marlin back to Devil's Island.

His grip tightened upon the .38 and he drew it closer to the torn front of his shirt.

Paco was elegantly dressed as always. Even in French Guiana he had managed to find excellent clothes but now he surpassed himself. His coat was of the best linen and the best cut. His trousers were pressed until the creases were sharp as bayonet blades. His shoes were so white they hurt the eyes on this brilliant tropical day. His cap would have been the envy of a British naval officer, so rakish was its slant, so shiny was its braid.

The insignia was strange to Lars. But it did not matter. Paco was a steward on a yacht, he supposed. But Lars wasted no thought upon Paco Corvino's present. The past was a dull throb in Lars Marlin's brain.

There, jaunty and well fed and reasonably safe, stood Paco, pleased with himself because the Law had just tipped its cap courteously to him. If that officer only knew Paco. . . .

Murderer, contraband runner, escaped convict. A man with no more conscience than a bullet, a man cool and deadly, masking a cunning brain with a winning smile.

5

Oh, yes, Lars Marlin knew all about Paco. It had been Paco who had changed Captain Lars Marlin into Convict 3827645. Paco had done that out of vengeance and now, thought Lars, the tables were turned. One bullet . . .

Lars looked again at the Law under the awning. His gaze went back to Paco and then beyond him, down the cool avenue to tall green and tan palms. Red roofs and white walls. Rugged, pleasant hillsides rising . . .

Once more his hand clenched on the .38. This revenge was sweet enough to repay any consequences. Too long he had dreamed of this moment. He pulled the .38 clear of his shirt, pressing back against the cold, harsh wall. Carefully he leveled the gun. He had no compunctions about the sportsmanship of this. Paco knew that someday Lars Marlin would find him.

The finger began to squeeze down on the trigger.

Laughter nearby jarred Lars Marlin's nerves. The world was ugly to him and this laughter was too gay. Two American girls and a youth had come into the range, approaching the shadowy place where Lars stood.

As the group passed Paco, the blithe Spaniard saluted the man and swept off his cap in a low bow to the ladies.

"Good afternoon, all. Good afternoon, Miss Norton," said the smiling Paco.

Lars looked at Miss Norton. He did not take his eyes away. He could not. It had been long since this homeless American had seen a woman of his own race. And this woman was no usual girl. Her hair was as yellow as the sun. Her graceful body was enough to make de Milo weep from sheer inability to hold those unhampered, lovely curves in marble.

6

"Good afternoon, all. Good afternoon, Miss Norton,"
said the smiling Paco.

Straight and clean and beautiful, she gave the spellbound and unseen Marlin something back, something he had lost in the swelter of heat and the ungodly cruelty of an alien prison camp.

Almost ashamed, he slid the .38 back into his shirt.

Her voice was low and clear. "We sail at midnight, Paco. Make certain you're with us."

"*Yes*, Miss Norton."

The group passed on. They were almost abreast of Lars now. In a moment they would pass within two feet of him. He sensed the presence of her companions but he had eyes only for Miss Norton. He had not heard laughter for years unless it was the wild laughter of madness.

Involuntarily he took off his cap as she passed. A supercilious, patronizing voice brought him back.

"Here, my man."

Silver clinked in Lars Marlin's cap. Blankly he glanced up at the donor. The youth was back between the girls, walking away. Lars looked at the fellow wonderingly. The man had been drinking, as his walk was exaggeratedly straight. Neat and flabby, he had no more character than a dummy outside a clothing store.

Lars Marlin took the *milréis* out of his cap and looked at it. His big, hard mouth curled with contempt. He threw the coin across the walk where an ancient, scabby beggar scooped it up avidly.

Lars looked back at Paco.

Not here. There were other ways. But meanwhile he must

not lose the man whom fortune had placed so kindly in his way.

Hesitantly, Lars stepped forward. The hot sun struck his half-bare back and showed the play of muscles through the shredded rag he wore. Beyond him Paco stood looking across the street, jingling coins in his pocket. In profile his face was hawklike and his ivory white teeth flashed like fangs. But, even so, he was pleasant to look upon.

He had been raised on the wharves of world ports without number, foraging with the rats, keeping the society of the drifting flotsam, appearing and disappearing, untraceable. He had developed a smile as armor and it was no deeper than the metal of a salade. And though he did not know his real name he had carefully developed the manners of an aristocrat. It was like Paco to stand in plain sight of the Law, smiling, secure and confident.

Lars came to a heavy stop on Paco's right. They were the same height but there the similarity ended. Lars was built strongly, hewed massively from granite.

Paco looked down at his feet and saw a blue shadow lying there. He saw the breadth of that shadow, how motionless it was, how broad the shoulders were. He saw the outlined tip of an officer's cap.

Paco knew without turning that Lars Marlin, whom he thought to be two thousand miles away in safe confinement, stood with him in the blazing light of the Brazilian sun.

It was not part of Paco's code to show shock. For all he

knew, the bullet he so well deserved might be on the verge of an eager trigger. Fear made Paco curl up like burning paper—but only inside. He was sick with nausea and his heart lurched heavily and began to pound in his throat.

Across the street stood the Law, beyond call. Paco must stand there and give no sign.

Only slightly congealed, only a little more false than before, Paco's smile was slowly turned to Lars.

Their eyes clashed. Dark orbs recoiled before the baleful certainty of Norse blue.

Lars did not move, but Paco sensed that he did. Lars was holding himself enchained and his hands, thumbs hooked into rawhide belt, were shaking slightly. Shaking, Paco knew, because they could already feel a man's breath damned up in his contracted throat.

But Paco smiled. He had no ace in his sleeve but he had a knife, strapped to his wrist in a sheath. He had only to jerk his arm and the knife would glitter in his palm, ready to strike.

Paco's voice was easily mocking. "So you came to Rio for me. If you had arrived tomorrow, I would have been gone. You always were lucky, Lars."

"I was lucky until I met you, Paco."

"How did you escape?"

"The same way you did." Lars Marlin's tones were heavy, monotonous, eating into Paco with far more effect than if they had been the ranting harshness of rage.

"Congratulations," said Paco.

"If you have a few minutes," said Lars, "I'd like to see you alone." Paco knew he meant the Law across the street. It seemed funny to Paco to be standing here, actually under the protection of the police.

"I don't think we have anything to talk over, Lars. If you need money . . ."

"Silver won't buy your life."

Paco was amused. "In the numerous times we have met, Lars, you have yet to come out a winner."

"That was yesterday. This is today. Shall we go to some quiet place, Paco?"

Paco shrugged. "I can understand that you might be angry about that Casablanca deal, but after all, Lars, you were the one who turned me over. Wasn't I entitled to take you along to French Guiana with me?"

"If you were, then I have some rights now," said Lars.

"Rights! Does an escaped convict babble about rights? See here, Lars. If you . . . Wait. You're branded now. You can't live inside the law. I've just had an idea."

"I am not interested in your ideas. Will you come or do I have to . . ."

A man in brass-buttoned whites stepped between them, facing Paco. Lars was annoyed at himself. At the first flash of gold he had recoiled in fear of police. But this was not police. The man was elderly. His rum-reddened face was flabby, filled with small broken veins. His hair was white as a bleached bone. He wore a captain's stripes and the insignia upon his cap matched Paco's.

"Sorry I kept you waiting," said the strange captain to Paco. "*They* won't take less than . . ."

Paco shot a triumphant glance over the old man's shoulder

11

to Lars. "Just a minute, Captain. I wish to present one of my old friends. A man who might be expected to help us." When the officer faced around, Paco, with a mocking wave of his hand, said, "Captain Simpson, this is Captain Lars Marlin."

Simpson's weak eyes showed his distrust. His freckled hand in Marlin's was cold and moist and weak.

Paco swept on. "Marlin is an old friend of mine, Simpson. We were together years ago on the *Moroccan Queen*. You recall the incident?"

Simpson was startled. He looked swiftly from Lars to Paco, and in an incredulous voice, cried, "You mean he's . . ."

Paco's smile was amused. "Yes. He just managed his escape from Devil's Island."

Simpson gasped and stared at Lars. The tattered giant's glare was hot enough on Paco to wither him. The mighty fists were drawn up in steel mauls.

But Paco's quietly laughing voice surged on. "I see you remember, Captain. It was all very interesting. You recall when the French authorities searched the *Queen* for contraband dope? They found it on me, of course. Marlin here gave them the first clue which fastened it upon me. And you remember what happened after that. It was discovered that quantities of it were in his cabin. He swore he did not know how they got there, those little tins. Naturally they packed him off with me. Lars here is a very persistent fellow. He tried three times to kill me in the Penal Colony. That scar you can see on his chest was given him by my knife on the third try. And now he is with us again. Good, kind Lars."

Simpson was opening and closing his mouth like a red snapper. He was struggling for air.

"And since," continued Paco, "we have a use for such a man, it might be well to include him in the *Valiant*'s crew. I shall draw up a paper and leave it in the bank here, to be opened in case of my death, and the authorities will know exactly where to find him. Is that agreeable, Simpson?"

"Good God, NO!" cried Simpson. "You're mad! You are telling him a thing no one should know except ourselves!"

"Nonsense," said Paco, grinning easily. "He knows that where he would find me, he would find contraband. He knows that is my weakness. And besides, Simpson, it will keep you from getting a notion to rid yourself of me."

Lars glanced across the street. The Law was still standing there, completely unaware of anything wrong in that quiet group across the pavement. It was all so lazily peaceful in this hot afternoon sunshine. No man—or at least no sane man—would take the siesta hour to plan death.

Lars studied Paco. He knew what to expect from the man. Paco was so plausible, so merciless, so much at his ease, that he was safe in any society. He classed murder with picking pockets.

And Lars knew another thing. Paco would find some way to direct the police to him if he failed to follow Paco's course. But in following that course, Lars knew that he could at last even up the mounting score. He could wait. He had learned to wait.

Lars knew that Simpson was a fool. Paco had duped

Simpson into playing a criminal role, using the man's natural weakness and greed. Lars also knew that Paco no longer needed Simpson. He sensed that because he knew the ways of Paco all too well.

"I . . . I shall have to consult Miss Norton," gasped Simpson. "After all, I am only her captain. Perhaps," he added hopefully, with an uneasy glance at Lars, "perhaps she will not consent to another crew member when there are no vacancies."

"She'll consent to anything I propose," smiled Paco.

"Someday she'll discover how wrong she is," said Simpson. "We won't be able to get away with this forever."

"But while we *can* get away with it, we can make our fortunes. What better means of transportation is there than the *Valiant*? Who would dare suspect Teresa Norton of smuggling? You are getting shaky, Simpson."

"What if I am?" said the captain, abruptly belligerent.

Paco shrugged. "Let it pass. Suppose you catch up with Miss Norton—she just went toward the quay—and ask her."

"I don't think I shall," said Simpson. Suddenly he began to whine. "You can't make me do this, Paco. After all, we know this man is an escaped convict. . . ."

"So am I," said Paco. "And so will you be someday. Get along and make the request."

"And if I refuse?"

Lars knew how dangerous was the ground on which Simpson stood. A soft, purring note had come into Paco's voice.

Again Paco shrugged that fatalistic Latin shrug. "Refuse, then. Come, we grow too serious. Let us go somewhere and have a drink and after that I'll file this paper at the bank."

14

He looked at Lars and the smile was uncertain for an instant. "No. I'll file that paper now, across the street. Wait here." Lars was helpless to stop this with three beneath the awning. Sullenly he watched Paco cross the pavement and enter the bank. He knew now he should not have delayed that bullet. He should have taken his chance when he had it, despite the risk. Lars and Simpson were uncomfortable together. Simpson considered Lars far beneath him and Lars considered Simpson a very low form of insect life. Simpson was a man who would betray an employer like the girl Lars had seen. He would sell out a trust for a pittance. He was weak and unintelligent. And though Lars might have warned Simpson, he did not. Simpson would not have taken the warning and the crime merited the punishment.

Paco came back, breezily jingling the coins in his pocket, smiling with good humor, walking elastically.

"And now, my uneasy companions," said Paco, "let us partake of refreshment."

"Sorry," said Lars slowly. "I'm afraid I'm not drinking with either of you."

Paco laughed merrily. "Still the same Lars! At least let us find you a good bed before we leave you. This afternoon I'll bring you news . . . No. I have a better plan. Too bad you do not possess a strategic mind, Lars. I might have been dead by now if you had. Simpson, meet me in an hour at the Café of the Captains."

Simpson grumbled about it but it was easily seen that he was glad to get away from the company he was in. In mutual disgust and distrust they parted.

15

Paco and Lars walked up the avenue between the palms and the white building fronts, proceeding silently for three blocks. As they turned down a side street toward a sailors' hotel, Paco grinned suddenly.

"Perhaps I wrong you, Lars."

"Perhaps."

"You seem to be falling into this with suspicious ease."

"Am I?"

"But I know you too well to suppose that you have changed your mind. You saw Miss Norton, didn't you?"

"Certainly."

"You always were a romantic fool, Lars. And there's the difference between us."

"I am not interested," said Lars.

"But I am," smiled Paco as they paced along toward a swinging sign. "That is the difference. You are a romantic fool and I am merely romantic. You allow scruples to stand in your way and thereby hamper yourself. Undoubtedly you were on the verge of potting me from cover this afternoon. But you didn't. Why? Because it would not have been sportsmanlike to shoot an enemy in the back, no matter one's opinions about that enemy. You probably thought you would go through with it, but you didn't. You never would have, no matter how close you came.

"Now I am different, Lars. I would have fired from cover and made my escape, sparing myself unpleasant entanglements such as those in which you now find yourself. You saw Miss Norton—I saw your face light up when I mentioned her name—and now you know that she is in danger from me. And that is making you walk ahead, wondering if you can help the first decent woman you've seen in years. The temptation to be near her in any capacity is too much to resist. You hope you can somehow kill me for what you think I have done to you and so you are willing to carry on and wait. You can wait, Lars. It is a good trick. One that I never learned. Here we are. We shall go in together. Your name is Lowenskold and you have been shipwrecked from the SS *Tatoosh* which sank off Cape Frio some days ago."

They passed through the lobby and the smiling, plausible Paco engaged a room for them both. There was nothing said about it. The clerk was of the opinion that Paco was a pleasant fellow.

They climbed the musty staircase and came to a room which overlooked a muddy patio. The place was as bare as a cell, and Lars dwarfed everything in it.

Lars sat down on the bed, Paco threw some bills on the table and grinned in Lars' direction.

"Go right ahead," said Lars. "But don't be under any delusions about this. I'm with you only so long as I can keep myself under cover. And paper or no paper, I'm telling you now, Paco, that your number is up."

Paco shrugged that Latin shrug of his. "We know each other, Lars. That makes it better. You know that I will kill you as soon as you are no longer useful to me. I know that you wish to kill me. We hate each other with great cordiality. We can work together, Lars."

Paco walked out and closed the door behind him. Lars stretched his tattered length on the bed and stared up at the ceiling, hands clasped under his neck.

A brown lizard, upside down against the plaster, was walking with vacuum-cup tread. The lizard stopped and began to circle an unwary black bug. The tongue flicked and the bug was gone.

CHAPTER TWO

"Simpson Is Murdered!"

L ARS MARLIN dozed but it was an uneasy twilight into which he entered. The white room was uncomfortably like a prison cell, though far better than those of French Guiana. The plaster walls were cracked jaggedly, suggesting nonexistent rivers of a nonexistent world peopled with moths, roaches and wandering, hungry lizards.

At each approach of footsteps, Lars would start up, realize where he was and then lie back. There was high danger in his being in Rio, but that danger was as nothing compared to the recent perils of flight. Even so, recognition would send him back to the mire of swamps and the living, feverish death of oblivion.

Lars was too tall for the bed—built for smaller Spaniards—to accommodate him. He was lying cornerwise, bare heels on the one chair. In repose his face was handsome in its way, more because of the strength it indicated than because of the regularity of features. His mane of yellow hair had grown long and tangled, and his jaw was unshaven. Had it not been for the clear intelligence of his eyes and the hardness of his body, he might have passed for a beachcomber.

Footsteps sounded in the corridor outside and he started up. But the sound died away and he lay back, wondering where Paco was. He doubted that Paco had gone to the Café of the Captains. He suspected Paco's errand.

He considered his position without any great concern. He was in a strange place, living under strange circumstances. Six years before, as master on the bridge of the *Moroccan Queen,* he would have mocked any soothsayer who had tried to tell them that at the end of these six years he would be lying in a sailor's flophouse in Rio, considering ways and means of killing a man and dreaming intermittently, when he dozed, of a girl with a free swing to her walk and a pleasant if slightly imperious smile.

But now that he was here, he was taking it quietly, as he had taken everything else Fate had doled out to him. His life had been a checkerboard of odd occurrence.

His father had died in the Grand Banks fleet, leaving a nine-year-old boy to look out for his mother and two sisters. Lars had looked out for them as handsomely as a New England fishing town and the pay of a sailor before the mast would allow.

At the age of fifteen, he had begun to pound out a reputation for himself with his sledgehammer fists. He had risen to a mate of a coasting steamer. He had sent three quarters of his pay home and had invested the remaining pittance in extension courses. He rose from mere trig to theory of equations. He slugged a course in maritime law until it flattened out into a diploma. He read until his arctic-blue eyes ached, burning the daylight with labor and the darkness with study.

At eighteen, Lars Marlin had his master's papers. At twenty-one he had his first command—a wallowing old tub running on a thin profit margin with sighing boilers and weary screw. With insight and left hooks he had made that hooker pay and men began to know that Lars Marlin was carving a place for himself in the watery world.

One determined characteristic carried him through, gave him a name. Once he made a decision he never changed it. Vacillation to Lars was the worst crime on earth. He drove straight ahead making his own destiny, afraid of nothing. He had a retaining mind, an observing eye and knowledge which came from the entire ladder of knowledge—from the wharves to the universities.

At twenty-four he had been given a Mediterranean command, and from the bridge of the *Moroccan Queen*, men hoped he would graduate to a swift transatlantic liner.

At twenty-five he had taken on one Paco Corvino as chief steward because the man was recommended so handsomely. And three months later the officials of Casablanca had discovered contraband on the *Queen*. Lars had pointed the finger at Paco and Paco, in retaliation, had pointed back to the bridge.

And now at thirty-one, with six years of hell behind him, he found himself lying in a third-rate hotel wondering about the best and quickest way to commit a murder.

It was dusk when Paco came back. He slid through the half-opened door and closed it as silently as he had opened it. He stood listening for an instant, breathing hard. Then he turned and sat down on the other bed.

He grinned at Lars. "Anybody call when I was gone?"

"No."

Paco's smile widened and his white teeth flashed. He was very relieved at this news. He got up and walked to the wash stand and began to wipe the grime from his hands. The water turned a faint pink color.

"You're sure nobody, not even a chamber boy, called?" he asked without turning.

"I'm sure. What have you been doing?"

"Fixing things up. Simpson was turning yellow. I can read men, Lars. You won't deny that. I had pushed him as far as I could make him go. He was about to go mewling to Miss Norton. You saw it."

"What kind of contraband?" said Lars, lying on his side. He could feel the hard ridges of the .38 under him and his eyes were examining the possible target.

"Heroin," said Paco promptly. "They're death on it in the States. Can't even get it through a doctor. Never take it myself but I hear it's good for the nerves—or bad for them. Prices are rocketing up north. But heroin is small stuff. Listen, Lars, would it surprise you to know that I have a way of making four million francs all in a lump? Within a month and with hardly any risk."

"I'm not interested in your plans," said Lars.

Paco laughed aloud.

"What's so funny?" demanded Lars.

Paco shrugged. He had evidently forgotten that he had already washed his hands, as he again approached the stand and repeated the process.

"This Miss Norton owns the *Valiant*?" said Lars.

"No. Her father does. He's Tom Norton, president of the Equatorial Trading Company. He can sign his name to a ten-million-dollar check and still stay on easy street. The *Valiant* is a good little ship. Eighteen hundred tons, Diesel-engined. Pretty swank."

"Is Norton aboard?"

"No. He turned it over to his daughter and her friends and told them to go have a good time. He probably wanted to get rid of Miss Norton—Terry, everybody calls her. She's hotheaded and boy, can she get mad."

"So you're operating against a girl. That's worthy of you, Paco."

"Of course it is," cried Paco. "What use have I got for these people with money and position? I hate them! And what a fine time I have laughing at them. They think I'm something pretty special because I've got better manners than they have, because I can wear my clothes better than their men can. They wonder about it just as though they were God's chosen children, the only graceful people on earth. They order me around now but one of these days . . ."

Paco was not smiling. He was bitter and the black jungle cat in him was plainly visible in his displayed fangs and hot black eyes. But he passed it over with a shrug and began to smile again. He was rubbing his hands very thoroughly with a towel as though to rid them of something.

Finally he nervously perched himself on the edge of the bunk and began to manicure his nails with a little silver set he carried. He was very particular about his hands, more particular than ever on this day. They were the hands of an artist, and Paco, in his way, *was* an artist.

"I suppose the police will be here soon enough," said Lars quietly.

Paco jumped and again the smile was gone. "How did you know?"

"I suppose you thought I'd miss the case of nerves you brought back. I hope they swing you for it."

"For what?" demanded Paco.

"For the murder of Captain Simpson."

Paco was up, shaking with fear and anger, glaring down at Lars who remained casually sprawled on the bed.

"I'm not pleased," said Lars. "Watching you hang would have its points, but I would find it unsatisfactory. You plan very carefully, Paco, but this time you missed a trick."

Paco did not move.

"You went out of here and down the hall to the rear of the building," said Lars. "Nobody saw you leave this hotel. You came back and nobody saw you enter."

"You spied on me!"

"No. I'm guessing. But I know that you intend to use me for a perfect alibi. Perhaps you even wanted to hang this extra millstone on my neck. I don't know about that. You have committed a crime which is perfect from the angle of the police. But you forget that I am badly wanted in French Guiana. If they send me back, I'm taking you with me. You felt too secure to remember that you are also badly wanted."

"You're a fool," said Paco, sitting down again. "As big a fool as always. We understand each other, Lars. You can't kill me. I would be foolish to kill you—at the moment. You came opportunely. I was tired of masking facts to Simpson. But you . . . You won't ever talk out of turn. Soon as you do, blowie, you're on your way back to French Guiana. Simpson is dead. Captains—American captains—are scarce in Rio. You are about to become the captain of the yacht *Valiant.*"

Lars smiled slightly. "What will I do for papers?"

Paco was not in the least perturbed. Looking his contempt for Lars, he reached into his spotless coat and pulled out a sheaf of papers.

"You think I would forget a detail like that? You can buy all the forged papers you want in Rio. I could get records making you anything from a French private to a Balkan king. In this case I got papers and records which show you are Lars Lowenskold. You were wrecked on the *Tatoosh,* a lumber schooner, which went down off Cape Frio ten days ago."

"Was there such a wreck?"

"There was. Give me credit, Lars. I'm smart. The *Tatoosh* went down with all hands including three unknown passengers. You are one of those passengers, on your way to take over the command of another vessel. Here are your papers."

"You think Miss Norton would swallow that?"

"She'll swallow anything I tell her," grinned Paco.

"And when the police come charging in here . . ."

"Unless you want to go back to French Guiana, you'll tell them I've been here all afternoon, sleeping."

Lars raised himself on his elbow. "Get me straight on this, Paco. I only want one thing. A chance to kill you and get away. It's fair to warn you. I'll take this job because I think I can queer your rotten scheme, whatever it is, and do the thing I've waited to do for so long. I don't want to see you swing. Your life is *mine*."

Paco grinned broadly. He got up and lit a cigarette and stood looking down at the muddy patio. At last he turned to Lars. "That's fair enough. If I thought for one minute you had the brains to best me, I'd die of shame. You won't talk. You don't want to rot in the Colony. And you won't kill me as long as you know that my death will cause those papers to be opened. I need you to captain the *Valiant*. You'll captain it and follow my orders."

Lars lay back and looked up at the lizards on the ceiling. "We'll know more about it later on, Paco."

CHAPTER THREE

Alias Captain Lowenskold

THE yacht *Valiant* plowed diamonds out of the turquoise channel, sweeping swiftly and gracefully past Fort Lage, so low the waves broke over it in bad weather, into the outer channel.

The flippant little ship, picking up knots, slapped the waves of its wake against the frowning walls of Fort Santa Cruz on one side and Fort São João on the other. It refused to be dwarfed by the heights to port and starboard, sailing impertinently out to sea with the Sugar Loaf rearing to the west and the Pico soaring all green and tan to the east.

Ahead lay the broad immensities of the South Atlantic, lined with long green swells and washed by a hot, damp wind. The starboard almost touched the Tropic of Capricorn and then the spinning wheel pointed the clipper bow northeast.

Captain Lars Marlin stood solidly on the bridge, the stirred wind cool against his shaven cheeks. The excellent drill of his white uniform felt like silk as it was pushed against him.

Outward bound, in command of a beautiful vessel, he reverently watched the wide-ranged pattern of clouds and waves. He knew he did not deserve this but, for the moment, the thought was submerged. He felt strong, able to contend with anything.

"Northeast by east," said Lars.

The yacht Valiant *plowed diamonds out of the turquoise channel, sweeping swiftly and gracefully . . .*

"Northeast by east. Aye, aye, sir."

The helmsman brought the wheel down a spoke and steadied it there. He was a good sailor and he had already given his respect to this tall, strong gentleman who had boarded the *Valiant* under such strange circumstances.

Lars turned and looked back toward Rio. It was all gone now except for the heights of the Carioca Range, growing dim and blue with distance. He could see the Hunchback and high, flat-topped Gávea—named because of its resemblance to a Portuguese square sail—and the outline of the "sleeping giant" as made by the entire range.

Lars smiled and faced away from it, looking again at the limitless horizons.

He heard footsteps behind him on the iron ladder. The sound broke into his thoughts and annoyed him. But he did not turn, hoping whoever it was would not come into the windswept wing. Lars did not want company.

The footsteps were light and carefree and suddenly all irritation dropped away and became a kind of electric thrill. He did not have to use his eyes to confirm the fact that this was Teresa Norton. During the past two weeks he had more than once experienced this feeling of unexplainable elation which came over him and blanked out everything sordid whenever he was with her.

When he knew she was within an arm's length of him he pivoted and saluted her. "We're off to a fair breeze, Miss Norton."

She smiled at him and placed her back against the rail. Her

29

yellow hair was blowing about her face and her eyes were as quick and pleasant and changing as the South Atlantic.

"How do you like the *Valiant*?" she said.

"She's a thoroughbred, Miss Norton."

"Of course you're used to bigger ships."

He wished she had not said that. It reminded him of this enforced masquerade. He managed a smile in return. "But not better."

She seemed to be studying him and he felt uneasy under her clear scrutiny. He knew she was interested in him but he supposed that it was the same interest a child would show to a piece of driftwood of queer design found upon the shore.

"You seem to be very happy about getting away from Rio," she said.

This jolted him. Could it be that she knew more about him than he suspected? Could Paco . . . No, she was just being polite.

She saved him his answer. "But then I suppose the loss of that promised job and the enforced stay in a dull town wasn't pleasant to a man of action like yourself."

"Thank you, ma'am."

"What for?" she asked in surprise.

He faltered and swiftly recovered. "Thank you for getting me out of that scrape. It's no joke to be stranded. A seaman who has been wrecked can get transportation to his ship's home port merely by asking the consul, but a captain cannot."

"I am glad I had the luck to find you after . . ." She was remembering Simpson and the short, pointless police investigation which had followed.

"I hope I'm not bringing you bad luck, Miss Norton."

"No. That's silly. Of course you aren't. You didn't know anything about me until after . . . after it happened. I doubt you knew the *Valiant* existed."

She was looking at the receding blueness of the ranges of Brazil and Lars watched her, glad to be able to do so without having to meet her eyes. It was hard to face that frank appraisal. He hated himself for not being able to tell her about this deceit.

"I have an uneasy feeling," she said at last, "that there was something more than personal enmity or robbery behind . . . Simpson acted strangely that day. He seemed to know something was coming. Two or three times he started to tell me something and then wouldn't. And now, although we're free of Rio, I can't help but . . . But this is all nonsense. There's no reason to worry you—indeed there isn't any reason anything will happen. This world is too well policed for piracy and we carry nothing valuable. Outside of yourself we have no new members in the ship's company and I have perfect faith in those who have been with me. Still . . ."

She shivered a little as though she was cold. The gesture had a strange effect upon Lars. He wanted to step close to her and put his arm around her and tell her that she needn't worry an instant about anything. He was there to see that nothing occurred. He was learning about this girl. She ruled those about her but she was kind. She trusted her friends and now she seemed inclined to rely upon Lars. She had a rare virtue in that she could talk to a man and make him feel at ease. Lars wished she weren't so beautiful.

31

She was worldly but not wise. She spoke of Paris and Moscow and Shanghai as carelessly as most girls talk about a party they have recently attended. Her knowledge of far lands seemed to be limited, however, to a strict upper strata. There was something engagingly childish about her enthusiasms.

"Nothing's going to happen," said Lars, almost gruffly.

She faced him again. Yes, he was right. She did rely upon him. That simple statement of his had momentarily wiped away her gloomy apprehensions.

Lars was in conflict with himself. He wanted badly to tell her exactly how he knew nothing was going to happen. He wanted to tell her that one Paco Corvino would one night be missing from the afterdeck of the *Valiant,* never to be seen again.

But you can't talk to a beautiful woman about coldblooded murder, no matter how certainly it concerns her.

He wanted to talk to her more, was glad of this chance, but he heard voices coming up the ladder. With a twinge of annoyance he watched two young women and the supercilious young man come out of the companionway.

"Oh, Kenneth," giggled a brunette named Alice, "you say the wittiest things."

"Oh, I don't know," said Kenneth, proudly.

"You do so!" challenged the other girl, a fluttery child called Rosey.

Alice came straight to Miss Norton. "Oh, Terry, you know what Kenneth just said?"

Terry, to Lars' disgust, seemed interested.

"He said . . . What did you say, Kenneth?"

"I said, 'If you were Sugar Loaf, I wish I was Pico.' Get it, Terry?"

Terry made a wry face. "That was awful, Kenneth."

"I thought it was pretty good," defended Kenneth.

Rosey took Kenneth's arm. "So did I."

"Aunt Agatha," said Alice, giggling, "refused to make a fourth at bridge after Kenneth redoubled six spades and set her last night. She says she has a headache. Won't you come down, Terry?"

"If our doughty mariner can run this ship without you," said Kenneth, "you'd save us all from dying of ennui."

Terry did not want to leave very badly. "Where's Ralph?"

"He's reading a book on big game hunting," said Alice, giggling. "He says he's going to Africa, just as though anybody ever goes to *Africa*. He says he's going to shoot a . . . What was it, Kenneth?"

"A wamphohitadile," said Kenneth.

Rosey laughed and looked adoringly at Kenneth. Alice shrieked. Terry suddenly looked sideways at Lars and saw that he was not smiling. He did not notice. He was watching Kenneth with amazement.

A quiet, unobtrusive laugh was heard behind them and Paco edged through.

"How was that one?" demanded Kenneth of Paco.

"A rare animal," said Paco, smiling. "Is it the one which drinks oysters and eats beer?"

Everyone laughed except Lars and the helmsman, who

concentrated upon his job. Lars noted carefully that Paco's
air took all the freshness out of his remark. He was being
flattering to Kenneth. Paco shot Lars a triumphant glance
which clearly said, "See, they think me most amusing. I can
wrap them around my finger without half trying."

Paco touched his cap to Terry. "Miss Norton, I have set
up the table and made ready the cards. In Rio I picked up a
new kind of sandwich which I would like you to try."

"Did you remember the champagne?" demanded Kenneth.

"Vat '79, wasn't it, sir?" said Paco.

"That's right!" cried Kenneth. "Paco, you're a mastermind.
You remember everything!"

"I try to please, sir," said Paco, smiling.

The group moved toward the companionway and Paco
carefully and politely aided Terry to descend the steep steps.
But Paco did not follow them below. He came back to Lars,
glanced at the helmsman to make certain the man was far
enough away, and then relaxed into his easy, confident grin.

"We're on our way," said Paco, waving his hand gracefully
back toward the sleeping giant. "By this time you've probably
changed your opinion of me. It's not everybody who could
keep the center of the stage around here. They don't brush
their teeth without asking me first. Aunt Agatha makes me
choose her books for her and Ralph makes me tell him about
strange ports where I've never been and . . ."

"I'm not interested," said Lars.

"No?" smiled Paco. "But you will be. Next time you're
around Miss Norton, get her started on the subject of titles."

"What titles?"

"Dukes and princes and earls. Alice and Rosey both have peerages in their cabins—or did until yesterday. They've got money but they haven't social position. Get it?"

"No. Get off the bridge."

"You will soon enough. I'm deep, Lars. You ought to know that by this time. Napoleon was a half-wit compared to me."

"Listen here, Paco," said Lars very quietly. "This is my bridge, no matter how I got here. And stewards walk lightly aboard my ships. Now get below."

Paco rocked on his heels and his grin grew in impertinence. Then he laughed aloud and turned toward the ladder. He stopped at the top and looked back. He laughed again and clattered down out of sight.

Lars faced the wind again and watched the changing hues of the sea. But the elation was gone from him now. A nagging, bitter wrath, which had been with him these many years, was blown into its full force.

He did not like his position. He was too much a man of swift decision and straightforward action to appreciate the sublety of the maze which was enfolding him. He only knew one thing. He had to keep near Paco if he ever wanted to even up the score. And he had to make sure that nothing happened to this girl.

True, if anything happened to Paco, it was the Penal Colony again for Lars Marlin. If he tried to upset Paco's game, Paco would risk everything to show Lars up as an escaped convict—he might even try to pin Simpson's murder on him.

Something was about to happen. Something was happening this very instant. But Lars knew his best chance lay in waiting.

35

As yet he knew nothing except that Paco had a way to make four million francs. He vowed the grinning Spaniard would never live long enough to spend them.

Lars hit the rail with a clenched fist. If he could only think of some way to destroy Paco without destroying himself!

CHAPTER FOUR

Paco's Strange Illness

A T eight bells in the evening, Lars was again on duty,
relieving First Officer Johnson. Johnson and the other
two mates were efficient enough, very average mariners, but
it was indicative of their lack of ambition that there was not
another master's ticket aboard the *Valiant*. They all had little
enough to say to Lars. He was a stranger to them and though
they could easily see that his seamanship was good, they
reserved judgment.

Lars Marlin's state of mind was not a calm one and his
natural silence, added to this, gave him a reserved air which
they mistook for austerity.

Comfortably plump Johnson gave over the bridge with a
salute and the single statement of the course and left. The
quartermaster was relieved by the same man who had been
steering on Lars' first trick.

Lars looked into the binnacle, contacted his lookouts and
then went into the wing to lean against the rail and look
forward into the velvet warmth of the night.

Lars had wanted this trick because the *Valiant* was still
close in, crossing the steamer lanes which led to Rio from
the north.

He felt the strangeness of his responsibility. He had, in
this command, the lives of these people to protect. But more

37

than that, he could not be certain just how or where Paco would strike.

He felt very uncertain about Paco in several ways. The amazingly debonair cutthroat had worked himself into the confidence of this entire party. They suspected nothing of his past operations and had no inkling of his present plans, whatever they were.

Paco's luck was wonderful. With the utmost carelessness he had committed a "perfect" crime. He would never be brought to book by the Rio authorities for that murder. The audacity of the crime was quite in keeping with Paco's past operations.

Simpson had been found in an alley with three inches of steel though his heart. No knife, no clues, no visible reason why Simpson had been killed.

Facing the police, Paco had been wide-eyed and innocent. Miss Norton's solid recommendation about Paco had completely blocked any effort on the part of the police to investigate Paco's past. It was the furthest thing from anyone's mind that Paco had done the murder. He had grieved realistically, had told Miss Norton gallantly that he would help her.

Lars writhed when he remembered how he had been introduced to Miss Norton for the first time. Paco had made him buy clothes suitable for the occasion. Paco had presented him with quite an air, saying he had good reason to know that Lars "Lowenskold" was an excellent officer. And Miss Norton, shaking his hand, had looked kindly upon Lars and had said, "Anyone Paco recommends is acceptable to me."

How could they be so blind to this Spaniard's deceit? Were his perfect manners the only things they judged him by?

Plowing through the dark seas and thinking his dark thoughts, Lars got through his watch. Brighton, the third, relieved him at midnight.

Lars had worked himself up to a high pitch of nerves. He knew he could not sleep. He wandered down the deck, past the salon. An automatic phonograph was playing dance tunes and the voices which rose above the music were gay and laughing.

Standing beside a bulkhead, Lars looked through the salon window, the yellow light showing up the hard lines of concern on his sturdy face.

Aunt Agatha, thin and sharp, was knitting, looking up from her place against the opposite window and peering at the card players over the top of her gold-rimmed glasses. Ralph was sunk deep into a soft chair, sitting on his spine, watery eyes devouring the open book he held. He was pale, loosely hung together. Lars could see the title of the volume even from this distance, the print was so large. Ralph was reading *Tigers I Have Faced*, and his shock of yellow hair was standing straight up. He was in Burma while the jungle depths of Brazil flowed silently by on their port.

Kenneth Lewis Michaelson was making witty cracks over his bridge hand. Rosey Laughton laughed, sometimes, before Kenneth had reached the nub. Alice Crichton and Terry joined in occasionally.

To Lars it was a very strange cargo. He dwelt little upon

the others. He was watching Terry's breathtaking profile. It made him shiver strangely.

She was like a princess to him. He could never hope to tell her that he loved her. The limit of his transgression would be to stand here and watch her in the darkness.

He had always thought the daughters of rich men would be spoiled and temperamental and he had not looked to find beauty and kindness and frankness in a woman with such a background. She seemed to understand human things.

A girl of her golden caliber could never suspect anyone around her of treachery because she was so incapable of it herself.

The heavy hand of worry clutched at Lars again. If he only knew what Paco had in mind! But he did not know. The blow might fall tonight, tomorrow, next month. And what would Paco do? Would he try to pirate this yacht? Who were his confederates and where were they?

Lars had not misspent his afternoon. Under the blind of wanting to inspect his ship he had cruised through the holds and quarters, probing into bails and cans and tanks. He had not known what he might discover and he had discovered nothing. He was satisfied that Paco's present plans did not include contraband. What devilish undertaking could net a man four million francs? Lars felt in his pocket and the keys he carried jingled faintly.

The trap outfits, including shotguns, were in his possession, at least. So were three riot guns and six rifles, standard equipment for a yacht used to cruising in the furthest of the seven seas.

He heard Kenneth say, "Kings *will* take tricks," as he snapped one down on the board. It was the last of his book and he grinned all around and began to figure up the score.

"Kings," said Rosey with a sigh. "Terry, someday you'll have to fix it so we can meet a king."

"I met one in Paris," cried Alice.

They had evidently heard about this before as they did not press her to enlarge upon it.

She seemed hurt about this. "I don't care. He *was* a king although he had never been on a throne. Georgia Austin married a prince, didn't she?"

"They're hard to find," said Kenneth.

"But so romantic," said Rosey.

Terry seemed to be interested in the subject, much to Lars' surprise.

The conversation took a turn upon the entrance of Paco. The Spaniard, with deep courtesy, entered from another passageway carrying a tray of drinks. Lars looked sharply at Paco. There was something wrong with his face. And then Lars knew. Paco was not smiling.

"Oh, Paco," said Alice, "have you ever met an earl or a king or something?"

Paco set the tray down. He did not answer but he smiled as though he knew a great deal he was not saying. Then his smile faded away and he went on serving.

"Why, Paco, what's the matter?" said Rosey. "You look so pale!"

Paco did look pale. His cheeks were sunken and there were weary lines about his eyes.

41

"Aren't you feeling well, Paco?" said Terry.

"A little out of sorts," said Paco mildly with much apology of gesture. "Sometimes a jungle fever I contracted in Indochina returns. It is said that one gets it and never wholly recovers from it. After five attacks . . ." He stopped and went on serving the drinks.

"After five attacks," urged Ralph, sitting up with interest on the words, "jungle fever."

"They say one dies," said Paco. "It's just a silly native superstition of course."

"How many does this make?" gasped Rosey, very interested.

Paco did not answer her immediately. He finished serving and then picked up his tray and came toward the door near Lars. He paused with his hand on the knob and gave them all a very tired smile.

"Five," said Paco, exiting.

They would have stopped him if his dramatic exit had been less well done. But it was too perfect a thing to spoil. They began to buzz about it.

Paco bumped into Lars and was startled. He saw who it was and gave Lars his customary triumphant grin. "Taking in the scenery, eh?"

"Let's get a look at you," said Lars abruptly. He turned Paco's face around to the light and touched a finger to Paco's cheek. Lars snorted. "Cigarette ashes and a lead pencil, huh?"

"Well?" said Paco. "Effective, if nothing else."

"That's a cheap way to gain sympathy."

"When I want your opinions," grinned Paco insolently, "I'll ask for them."

He went on down the deck to his stateroom.

Lars looked into the window again and heard Aunt Agatha saying, "Poor boy. He did look tired. Perhaps if I gave him some sulphur and molasses . . ."

Lars went to his own room. He was puzzled as he took off his cap and jacket. He threw them on the bunk and then sat down in a wicker chair beside the open door and stayed there watching the horizon tip up and down. It was a faint horizon, the sea ceasing only where the brilliant stars began.

He sat there pondering for hours, knowing well enough that he should be getting some sleep. But he could not sleep. Death was hovering over this yacht. He could sense the beat of its black wings.

At four-thirty a sailor came to his door and started to knock. Then he saw Lars sitting just inside.

"Sir, Miss Norton says for you to come quick."

Lars reached for his jacket and cap. "What's the matter?"

"It's Paco, sir. They're in a terrible stew below."

"What's wrong with Paco?"

"Looks like he's going to weigh anchor for the next world, Captain."

Lars snorted. He went down the ladder to the lower deck and saw that the salon was brilliantly illuminated. Terry, in a silken negligee, was waiting for him at the door.

"Come quickly," said Terry. "It's Paco."

She led him down the deck to Paco's room. All the others were there, looking sad and standing nervously around. Paco was lying listlessly in his bunk, staring straight up at an I-beam above as though unaware of anything that was happening.

43

"Do something," pleaded Terry.

Lars had to carry through. He stepped to Paco's side and took the Spaniard's wrist, feeling the pulse. He received a shock. That pulse was very slow, almost stopped. Could it be that Paco was actually dying?

Lars felt cheated as he scowled down at the patient. Dying quietly in bed, was he?

Paco turned his head slightly. His eyes were glazed and his blue lips were clenched tightly as though in agony. But he managed a word. "Lars," whispered Paco. He tried again. "I'm glad . . . you came, Lars."

Aunt Agatha began to weep loudly.

Lars frowned. There was something wrong about all this, slow pulse or not. "What's the matter with you?"

"Don't be so harsh," protested Terry. "He's *dying*."

Paco touched Lars' hand feebly and tried to smile. "Goodbye, shipmate."

Aunt Agatha couldn't stand it. She had to leave. Rosey and Alice were weeping silently. Ralph looked awed, knowing well what these jungle fevers could do to a man.

"Miss Norton," whispered Paco.

She came to his side. "Yes, Paco."

"You're so dim," whispered Paco. "I . . . I can't see."

Rosey and Alice fell into one another's arms and sobbed. Terry's eyes were bright with tears.

"Miss Norton," said Paco, "I am a Catholic and there is no priest. Tonight . . . tonight I knew I was going. I wrote my confession and . . . and several letters. I want you to take care of them for me. All . . . all my papers are under my pillow. Take . . . them."

With a trembling hand she sought out the packet and held it. Paco collapsed. His eyes, wide open, staring at the ceiling. Something rattled in his throat.

Ralph, who knew what to do in such cases, pulled the sheet up over Paco's face.

They turned out the light and silently filed from the room.

Lars followed the others into the salon. He looked long at them, marveling at the way they carried on in memory of the little blackguard.

Finally he stumbled up to his cabin.

CHAPTER FIVE

The Resurrection

A T eight bells that morning, Lars was again on duty, by choice. He wanted to be busy. He felt angry with the world at large after what he had witnessed in the dawn.

But his woes were not yet complete. He had not been on watch a bell before Terry and Aunt Agatha came up on the bridge to see him.

"Captain," said Terry, almost reprovingly but very sad, "Why didn't you tell us?"

"Tell you what, ma'am?" said Lars.

"About Paco. You were his friend. You must have known who he was. Or did he swear you to secrecy?"

"I don't know what it's all about," said Lars.

"Young man," sniffed Aunt Agatha, "you certainly must have known. Such a dear, sensitive boy as Paco . . . " She wept.

"We will have to put in to the nearest port," said Terry.

"What's happened?" demanded Lars. "Can't we bury him at sea?"

"At sea!" said Aunt Agatha in amazement. "Bury a *prince* at sea?"

Lars scowled. "I'm sorry, ma'am. I don't understand."

"It was not right of us, of course," said Terry. "But Ralph and Alice kept insisting and we finally looked at his papers to find out whom he wished to notify. And this is what we found."

She handed Lars a packet and he opened up the first sheet. It was an ornate birth certificate which proclaimed to the world that Enríque Mendoza José Jesús Jorge Christofo de Mayal, of the House of Habsburg-Bourbon, had been born to the world.

Lars blinked at it. He took another and found that it was not yet opened, but was sealed with the arms of Aragon. Another was addressed to Alphonse XIII. Other sealed packets, with directions for dispatch followed. They were most imposing.

But the payoff, to Lars, was the note to Miss Norton which read, in part, "I regret this necessary deception after your great kindness and wish you to have some part of the monies I have hidden in French Guiana. (Signed) Enríque Mendoza José Jesús Jorge Christofo de Mayal, Prince of Aragon."

"You see," said Terry, "we must take him to the nearest port so that he can be buried with fitting honors. The poor fellow was driven out of his own country and had to take refuge among us and it is enough that he die unknown without burying him in that fashion. I . . ."

"Have you looked this up in a peerage?" demanded Lars. "There's some mistake! He's Paco Corvino, a—"

He stopped himself in time. To confess Paco's complete identity would be to ruin himself.

Terry was very cold to him. "It is not good taste to doubt the dead."

Aunt Agatha was wholly hostile on the instant. "The idea!" she sniffed, and tottered down the ladder to the main deck.

Lars was left to his amazement. What was this all about? And with Paco dead . . . What good could it do anyone now?

He moodily saw his watch through and at noon he finished his notes and went down to see if there were any further orders. He had already changed the course and speeded up for Pernambuco.

In his commodious cabin, at one, he sat down to eat his luncheon in solitary gloom. His appetite was small, completely taken away by the knowledge that Paco, ex-convict, dope-smuggler and multi-murderer, would be buried as he had lived, in complete deceit.

He could not dispel the lowering cloud of apprehension which closed gradually in upon him. Something was wrong with all this. The danger had not ceased. He felt it had just begun. A nameless premonition of disaster hung around him. Paco, certainly, was not through with this ship and Miss Norton. But there was no arguing the slowness of the wavering pulse and the death rattle he had heard in Paco's throat.

Bleakly, he hunched over his laden board and stared unseeing at the shining riot guns and rifles in locked racks on his walnut wall.

Had Paco made some rendezvous with criminals at sea?

Lars reproached himself for not acting in Rio. But how could he have done anything without bringing about his own return to the Penal Colony? Certainly a man owed himself some protection.

Shock-haired Ralph knocked on the door and Lars bade

him enter. Ralph Norton would have been handsome had he thought more about his personal appearance and less about his dreams. He was younger than Terry—Lars judged about eighteen.

"This is a pretty awful thing," said Ralph, lying back in the captain's easy chair and shoving his long legs out before him. "I'll bet you feel pretty bad about losing your pal, huh?"

Lars thought it better not to answer that.

"The whole ship is in an uproar," said Ralph. "Nobody had the least idea Paco was a real prince. Aunt Agatha will never get over making him wait upon her. Think of it! A real prince all the time. The girls feel pretty silly and pretty sad over the way they talked about wanting to meet princes when they had one right there."

"Ever think that might be a fake?" said Lars.

"A fake!" cried Ralph. "Why should it be a fake? Good God, the man wouldn't own up to it until he was dying, would he? And a man on his deathbed wouldn't tell a lie. There'd be no point in it."

"That is what is worrying me," said Lars.

"What?"

"Nothing. I suppose Terry will radio the news this afternoon."

"She can't," said Ralph. "Those documents are a sacred trust. She isn't supposed to let anybody know about it until those letters he wrote have been placed in the right hands. Terry keeps her word. You don't seem very excited about it."

Lars speared a potato with his fork and ate it.

"Wasn't he your best friend?" persisted Ralph. "He said he was."

"Sure," said Lars. "My very best friend."

Ralph missed the irony. "I get it. You're taking it big. Sure you would. A fellow like you who's been all around wouldn't break down or get excited. Say, this ship is sure getting its share of dead men. First Simpson and then Paco. Wonder who'll be next? These things run in threes, you know."

"Do they?" said Lars.

"Sure. Everything I read says they do. Railroad wrecks and drownings and things. Of course there'll be three."

Ralph found it very unsatisfactory to try to talk to this big blond fellow who had come into the Norton employ. For the space of a minute he scrutinized Lars. Here was a man, thought Ralph, who had seen things and been places. He was toughened and could be expected to put up a mean fight against anything from a lion to a pirate crew. He ended up by respecting Lars' reticence. Ralph got up.

"Gee, I sure wish you'd told us Paco was a prince, Skipper. You'd have saved the ladies a lot of worry about the things they didn't do. Well, see you later."

He did not get out of the door. Kenneth charged through the opening and collided with him. Kenneth was too excited to launch into any preliminaries. He threw his news into the room as though it were a hand grenade.

"He's alive! A couple sailors just went in to dress him up before we made port and they found his heart was still beating! Now what the hell do you know about that!"

Lars put down his fork and looked at the racked riot guns. The keys were sharp against his thigh.

"Paco's alive?" cried Ralph excitedly, as he came up recovering from the collision. "Gee whiz, lemme see him!"

Kenneth was already on his way out. He was babbling to Ralph, "His pulse was clear stopped last night. I felt it myself! And now he's breathing and he's got some color in his cheeks. Good God, Ralph, do you realize we've got a real, live prince aboard the *Valiant*?"

Lars went over to his desk and sat down. He opened a series of drawers until he found the cartridges which fitted the guns. He checked them and then locked them up. He examined his .38 and found it in good order. He slid it into his waistband and smoothed his crisp white jacket over the bulge it made.

He went to the racks and made certain that he had the right keys. He locked them securely and then placed his keys in the pocket nearest his .38.

He went back to his desk and sat down facing the door, cap pulled down hard, mouth tight with anger.

"Damn him," said Lars venomously. "I might have known. Arabian *benj*! He dared take the risk of dying from it just to slow down his black heart. God knows what he'll do with this new power."

Join the Stories from the Golden Age Book Club Today!

Yes! Sign me up for the Book Club (*check one of the following*) and each month I will receive:

○ One paperback book at $9.95 a month.
○ Or, one unabridged audiobook CD at the cost of $9.95 a month.

Book Club members get FREE SHIPPING and handling (applies to US residents only).

Name   (please print)

If under 18, signature of guardian

Address

City   State   ZIP   Telephone

E-mail

You may sign up by doing any of the following:

1. To pay by credit card go online at www.goldenagestories.com
2. Call toll-free 1-877-842-5299 or fax this card in to 1-323-466-7817
3. Send in this card with a check for the first month
   payable to Galaxy Press

To get a FREE Stories from
the Golden Age catalog check here ○
and mail or fax in this card.

Thank you!

#1 New York Times Bestselling Author
L. RON HUBBARD

Subscribe today!
And get a FREE gift.

For details, go to www.goldenagestories.com.

For an up-to-date listing of available titles visit www.goldenagestories.com

BUSINESS REPLY MAIL
FIRST-CLASS MAIL   PERMIT NO. 75738   LOS ANGELES CA

POSTAGE WILL BE PAID BY ADDRESSEE

GOLDEN AGE BOOK CLUB
GALAXY PRESS
7051 HOLLYWOOD BLVD
LOS ANGELES CA 90028-9771

CHAPTER SIX

Unlucky Latitude

ALL day the glass had been falling. The sea calmed until it was a stiffly bending sheet of gray iron. The only wind which stirred was that made by the *Valiant,* and this wind was a sluggish thing as though the ship struggled through a vast area of invisible glue.

From horizon to ominous horizon, no cloud stood alone, but the blue had become discolored until it was no color at all. And millimeter by millimeter, the glass continued its inexorable course down past the false markings of "Storm."

There was no storm here. Only a vast, crouching space of quiet sea and unmarked sky. But there would be a storm. Lars Marlin could feel it as certainly as he could feel the slow roll of the deck beneath his solidly planted feet.

Johnson, corpulent and common, came at eight bells in the afternoon to relieve Lars. He looked at the chart which lay with stubbornly curled edges upon the charting table and placed a pudgy finger near the cross which Lars had just made.

"South latitude thirteen," said Johnson, as near as he ever came to a joke. "We won't find any luck around here. God, I can't even breathe it's so hot."

"When the first blast hits, I'll be on the bridge. If I'm not, call me."

There was something in Lars' granitelike expression and

something in his voice which caused Johnson to salute and say no more.

Lars stepped out of the chart room and into the bridge wing. He stared out over the immense sameness of wind and water which blended into a sullen murk. His undershirt, beneath his stiffly starched exterior, was pasted hotly to his lean ribs.

He was waiting for something, he seemed to know that the something was coming. Inactivity had worn his nerves paper-thin and even his great stolid calm was on the verge of cracking.

He would welcome the coming violence of this blow. But now the sea was dead and the air was too thick to breathe.

He heard footsteps coming up to the bridge, careless, confident steps. He turned and saw Paco rise in sections to the level of the bridge deck.

Paco was grinning. He had changed subtly. There was less of furtiveness about him, more of command. He was dressed to his part as Prince of Spain. He wore Kenneth's clothes and looked better in them than Kenneth's spinelessness ever could. Rakish yachting cap, silk shirt, muffler of silk with small figured anchors of blue in it, correct trousers and spotless shoes. The whiteness of his attire set off the swarthiness of his features.

Lars stood solidly and watched Paco approach, face impassive but thoughts all focused on Paco's heart. The blue patch pocket made an excellent target.

"Well, am I good or am I good?" said Paco. He came to a halt, lit a monogrammed cigarette and flipped the match down into the dead sea. He faced Lars, grin widening. "For two days I've raised hell about them opening those letters before they were sure I'd passed to the Great Beyond and now I got them eating out of my hand. Did I tell you I was a genius?"

Lars looked his contempt.

"Don't you believe it even yet?" said Paco in mock surprise. "Why, Lars, that's ungrateful of you. After all I've done! And you know, of course, that I'll see you get entirely free of French officers. Oh, yes, of course, Lars. And haven't I built you up to Terry?"

"It's *Terry* now, is it?" said Lars.

"Sure," said Paco. "She fell for this prince gag like a ton of bricks. I'm on easy street. As soon as she carries out my orders—"

"Your orders? Are you ordering this ship now, too?"

"Certainly I am!"

"And where are we going?"

Paco grinned. "You'll know soon enough. Terry and the rest are 'thrilled to death' about it. Quite an adventure for them."

"You've still got me on the bridge, Paco."

"Is that a threat?" smiled Paco. "I think you'll go along with me—unless you want to land back in the swamps. It'll be Madame Guillotine next time. And by the way, Lars, it's not Paco now. After this, address me as 'Your Highness.' I think I shall have to require that of you."

Lars clenched his fist and Paco saw it without any change of countenance.

"I wouldn't," said Paco.

"You're taking this yacht to do your dirty business for you?" said Lars.

"Of course. I might add, Lars, that you would be wise to follow orders. Everything and everybody is on my side now. Even you!" He laughed amusedly at this and turned and went down the ladder and out of sight.

Lars looked back at the sea again. The keys to the gun racks were hard and sharp against his thigh. But he knew too well that any move he made would result in his sacrificing his own life.

He stood there for an hour, though he knew he was off watch and would need a short sleep to take his night trick. And at the end of that hour his reverie was cut short by a white swirl of skirt to his right. He had not heard Terry Norton approach.

He whirled about, startled for an instant. Then he saluted gravely. And then he saw something in her expression which alarmed him a little. She was very cold and formal—and could that be distrust in her beautiful face?

"Yes, ma'am?" said Lars.

"I have orders for you, Captain Lowenskold. Since discovering the real identity of Prince Enríque, we have made a change of plans. As we are a yacht we can enter ports at random."

Lars hesitated. He knew this was far from the right time to tell her anything but he thought that if he could give her some slight warning . . .

"Miss Norton, are you sure about Paco?"

Her tones were ice. "You mean His Highness?"

"I mean Paco Corvino. Miss Norton, I've got a hunch—"

"Are you, by any chance, trying to discredit him after seeing those certificates? Really, Captain Lowenskold, His Highness was right."

"About what?" demanded Lars.

"About you. I think it only right to tell you that he has discovered some things about you which are not very flattering to your character, and if he had known them he never would have recommended you as captain after poor Simpson's death. If you are trying to undermine my faith in His Highness, save yourself the breath. I came to give you orders."

The way she said that cut Lars deeply, gave him clearly to understand the fact that he was presuming when he considered himself higher than a butler aboard the *Valiant*.

"As you can navigate and as you are the only man with a master's license here, and as Johnson long ago refused command because he neither wants it nor has a ticket, you shall remain in your present status. However, any false step will bring your downfall with great quickness."

Stiffly, shivering with rage, his face white, Lars said, "You came with orders."

"Yes. You are to proceed to Cayenne."

"*Where?*"

"Cayenne, French Guiana."

"But, Miss Norton—"

"Are you going to obey my orders?"

Lars saw the futility of trying to interfere and the question blazed like lightning through his brain. What devilish scheme had Paco thought up? Why did Paco, ex-convict, want to place himself in the jaws of the Penal Colony once more?

"Are you going to obey?" said Miss Norton commandingly.

Lars turned on his heel, jaw set, eyes stubborn.

He entered the chart room.

"Mr. Johnson. We are changing our course for Cayenne. What is our position?"

"Latitude thirteen, sir. You saw it yourself an hour ago."

"Yes," said Lars in a voice as dead as the calm. "I saw it myself."

He picked up the dividers and stood looking at the widely spread chart and then, with a vicious snap of his hand, he speared the dot which was Cayenne. The dividers stuck there, quivering.

CHAPTER SEVEN

Coffins for the *Valiant*

AT Cayenne, Lars Marlin refused to cross the entrance to the harbor, dropping hook in the deep-water anchorage, six miles from the quays. The shallow entrance would only take fourteen feet but the *Valiant*, with the tide, could have managed that.

Swinging at her chain, bathed in the steaming sunlight of morning then, the *Valiant* awaited the return of the shore party which had left with the coming of the sun in a swift speedboat.

Lars nervously paced his cabin. He could not bring himself to spend too long a time upon the bridge. Every scraggly tree in the water seemed to possess eyes and every wave which slapped the *Valiant*'s white hull cried out that the shore knew he was there.

He stopped from time to time at the wide port of his big cabin to stare out through the harbor mouth, over the blue surface of the quiet bay and at the white and red town. Sight of Mt. Cépéron filled him with nausea. On it perched Ft. St. Michel. They could see the *Valiant* from up there.

He could place the governor's house even at this distance and could see the black rectangle which was the Place d'Armes.

Every landmark of the port shouted death to Lars Marlin.

Even his great strength was small beside the inexorable might of the French. His body cringed as it remembered the raw weight of irons and the oozing slime of the swamps. Past his eyes slouched a line of men in chains. One of them fell, to be dragged along by the rest—until the guards found that he was dead and cut him loose to throw the body into the sluggish, cayman-infested river.

A boat, still far off, was coming toward the *Valiant,* flying the tricolor. It was an official boat. Lars gripped the sill, watching.

A sound made him whirl. It was Ralph, and Lars had a difficult time trying to mask his terror.

"I guess they aren't ever coming back," complained Ralph, scratching his shock of upstanding hair. "They've been gone for hours!"

"You didn't go with them?" said Lars, knowing it was a foolish question even before he said it.

"No. They said I was one too many for the speedboat. They just didn't want me, that's all. All my life I've wanted to see the Penal Colony and they wouldn't let me go."

"Maybe you can make it tomorrow."

"Naw, we won't be here tomorrow. I wish they hadn't been so doggone mysterious about it. His Highness was going around like he was wearing gumshoes and a false mustache. He's up to something pretty smart, the prince."

From the first, Lars had not been able to believe that Paco would dare set foot again upon this shore. Certainly, it had been years since he had escaped. There had been no chase, even then. They had found a corpse and had named it Paco

Corvino and the incident was closed. They would not be expecting a guest of Miss Terry Norton's to be Paco Corvino. He looked different, too, now that he was well dressed and well fed. Still . . .

"What were they going to do?" said Lars.

"That's what makes me mad. The only chance for some excitement and they won't let me in on it. They've got a good plan. Pac . . . I mean His Highness is getting Terry to tell the authorities that she has come to request the removal of the bodies of four Americans who have been buried down here. A national gesture, y'understand. They'll make it pretty touching. And then somehow, His Highness says he is going to put his jewels and money into those coffins and bring them aboard that way. Ain't it a pip of an idea?"

"They can't get away with it!"

"Sure they can. These four Americans were flyers on an expedition and they died down here. His Highness knows all about it. They weren't convicts. So Terry is going to remove the bodies and take them home in state. It's pretty nifty, isn't it?"

"Sure," said Lars faintly. "Pretty nifty."

He turned back to watch the approach of the government launch. If only some official would recognize Paco. But then, that was too much to hope for. And if Paco was recognized, would he squeal on Lars? Sure he would. Hadn't he told Miss Norton a pack of lies to discredit the captain already?

"Why did she listen to the idea in the first place?" said Lars.

"Why not? It's lots of fun and, besides, isn't he an honest-to-God prince? Say, what'd you say about His Highness to Terry last Thursday that made her so mad?"

"Was she angry?"

"And how!"

"She's foolish to try to go through with this."

Ralph had not missed Lars' tenseness. "Say, what are you so jumpy about?"

"I didn't get much sleep during that blow."

"Oh. About time they were coming back. There's a boat. What is it?"

"You'd better go below, Ralph," said Lars, "and tell the gentleman in it that I'm on the bridge. Would you?"

"Sure," said Ralph. "But what is he?"

"Port captain, that's all. Captain Delal."

"You know him?"

Lars quickly shook his head and Ralph went out, puzzled. He turned. "How do you know his name?"

"It's in the *Coast Pilot*," said Lars evasively.

Ralph closed the door, and soon after, Lars heard the small motorboat putting at the gangway. He went to his mirror and looked at himself. He put on his cap and straightened up his blouse. Nervously he wiped the sweat from the palms of his hands.

Captain Delal came in without knocking. He was a short little Frenchman, proud of his small mustache and his debonair manner. "Captain Lowenskold? I've got a few clearance papers for you to sign. If you weren't a yacht, there'd be plenty of red tape, but Norton's a power down here." He spoke in slangy Colonial French, speaking no English. He had his black interpreter with him, but before he could put the words into

Barbados English, Lars, unwittingly, had almost answered in *prison French!*

"Merci, Capitaine Delal, je . . ." Lars stopped himself. Swiftly, he added, "I speak a little French. Served on French boats once. You said some clearance papers?"

But Captain Delal was looking strangely at Lars. "Pardon me, *m'sieu*, but haven't you called at this port before? Your face is familiar somehow."

Lars knew his face had been before Captain Delal in the past. He had been detailed to a harbor survey once.

"You must be mistaken," said Lars.

"But one is not likely to forget a fellow with shoulders so big and hair so very light. Yes, I have seen you somewhere." He puckered his brows, trying to recall.

"I am sure the captain must be mistaken unless he once lived in Marseille."

"No, never saw the place. Let me see. I swear, Captain Lowenskold, I even remember your voice. But that's silly, isn't it? My memory is playing me tricks. Here, the papers."

Lars sat down at his desk, after offering the captain a chair. A steward came in with glasses and bottles and set them down, carefully withdrawing. Delal poured himself a drink and sipped it with compliments on its quality.

"Quite in keeping with Norton's reputation," said Delal. "It isn't every day— Say, are you certain you've never been here before?"

Lars had been speaking in as correct French as he could muster, even injecting an American accent into it. "No. At times the memory is very odd, isn't it. But perhaps some other man looks something like me."

"Yes, that's possible. Yes . . ." He watched Lars for several minutes until Lars had finished with the papers. And then Lars handed the sheets across and got up to show that the interview was over. Delal did not rise.

"I think I know," said Delal with a relieved smile, pleased that he had recalled. "You look something like . . . pardon me, no offense, you know . . . a fellow named . . . let me see . . . Oh, yes. Of course! Marlin. Lars Marlin. And that's a coincidence. He had the first name of Lars, too."

Lars could not trust his voice. He saw Delal's gaze wander until it discovered the framed master mariner's license on the wall. He thought he saw the glance narrow.

"Well," smiled Captain Delal, rising, "I shan't clutter up your cabin longer. I have lots of ships to inspect."

He put the papers in his valise and handed it to the interpreter. They stepped out to the deck and the black raised an umbrella over the captain's head.

Delal's handshake was flabby and his smile insincere. "Hope to see you again, sometime, Captain."

"Of course," said Lars. "Glad you came."

The pair went down the ladder and soon Lars heard the motorboat putting as it put off. He watched it cross a space of water to a nearby freighter which was unloading to lighters in the stream.

Exhausted by the nervous strain, Lars sat down in his chair. He knew too well that when Delal got ashore he would mention this strange coincidence. The officials would think it best to check this master mariner's license on the wall just as a matter of form. Delal had made a mental note of those numbers and signatures, all false.

And shortly the whole French world would know that no such license had ever been issued. They would know that the captain of the *Valiant* was Lars Marlin, escaped convict!

In a short space of time he had hold of himself again. He took a drink from the tray and followed it with another. He could only hope that the checkup would be made weeks hence, though he knew that radios speeded such things.

At dusk he heard a tug bumping the side of the *Valiant*. He went into a wing and looked down.

The speedboat streaked in a wide white curve to the gangway and the party came aboard, Paco smiling and confident in their midst. It was in keeping with his insolence to get away with a call like that.

Lars transferred his attention to the lighter. Johnson was already taking orders for the loading. Four American flags were draped over four coffins.

Paco paused on the main deck and saw Lars above. Paco grinned and passed on.

Shortly, as the first coffin came swinging up over the rail and down into the hold, Miss Norton came to the bridge.

"Captain," she said coldly, "you will please proceed immediately for Lisbon."

"We did not clear for Lisbon but New York."

"I will fix that. You will please pay attention to your duties only. Lisbon."

Lars saluted stiffly and went into the chart room. He

whistled down the tube to his engineer and gave him his orders.

The last coffin was swinging high into the air, inboard and down. The tug was putting off, black smoke rising in a cloud about the *Valiant*.

CHAPTER EIGHT

Paco's Contraband

THE Canary Islands lay low on the horizon, far to starboard. The bows of the *Valiant* rose regularly to knife back into the easy swell. The throbbing Diesels drove tirelessly. All was well, to all appearances, aboard the yacht.

And yet, day by day, Lars Marlin's tension had grown. He had no slightest inkling of the contents of those mysterious coffins and Paco had volunteered no information to anyone about them. The contents were gold and jewels. The ship believed that. But just because Paco said so, Lars did not.

Lars stayed with his bridge. He was plainly *persona non grata* on the lower deck. Silence fell whenever he went down—and he had soon stopped going.

Only young Ralph, with his dreams of adventure, came to pass any time. A deep, dark past added to Lars Marlin's attractions as far as Ralph was concerned.

Lars was standing a watch, looking toward the Canary group to check his bearings, when Ralph came up that afternoon.

"Captain," said Ralph complainingly, "there's a sneak thief on board this ship. How do I go about catching him?"

Lars turned slowly. "A sneak thief? What's gone?"

"Well, I've had an idea for a long time I was going to go to Africa and shoot me a couple lions and I've been collecting guns."

"Guns?" And from Lars the word sounded like an exploding cartridge.

"Sure. I had three good rifles. A twenty-five-twenty. A Scho, a 9-mm Mannlicher and a couple automatics and some shells. Sis didn't know I'd been buying them here and there, so I don't dare tell her about it. You know how women are. Aunt Agatha wouldn't like it either. But I had them hidden away and now they've disappeared."

"How long has it been since you saw them?"

"That's it. Just this morning. And when I went back just now to clean up my Schoenauer, the locker was empty. Every bandolier was gone!"

"I'll take care of this," said Lars. "Do me a favor, Ralph, and don't say a word to anybody about this."

"Sure, but . . ."

"Our lives may depend upon your silence."

This statement sent Ralph back off the bridge, gaping and blinking. It sounded harsh and real, as though something was going to happen very shortly.

But nothing happened for the rest of the watch or during the eight-to-midnight. And then Paco stepped out of his cabin with a swift glance about him.

Far down the moonlit deck, Lars was standing in the shadow of a lifeboat. He had been there for three hours, certain that Paco would come forth sooner or later. And now that Paco had appeared, Lars knew there was something wrong.

Paco walked down the deck, passing from shadow to shadow, away from Lars, continually on the watch.

No one appeared to block Paco's furtive way. Lars waited

until Paco had rounded a bulkhead and then started forward with swift stride to overtake him.

When Lars reached the corner, Paco had vanished into the emptiness of the forward well. But a companionway was open, the only possible place Paco could have gone in so short a space of time.

Lars reached the top and started down, silently and carefully. The blackness of the hold engulfed him. Those coffins were down here.

The place was not large as it was needed only for ship's stores. But again Paco had vanished.

Lars slid behind a tall pile of hawser and crouched there, listening. At first he could hear nothing except the ordinary ship sounds, but at last he could sort out the pulsating engines and the waves and the familiar creaks and groans of a moving vessel. There was another sound here in this hemp and tar laden interior. The buzz of whispering voices!

Quickly, Lars crept closer. He could see a yellow aura of light as he approached. A lantern was masked by a barricade of bales.

An inch at a time, Lars crept up the incline of stacked boxes until he could peer over the upper rim and down.

Four coffins, side by side, were open.

Four bearded men and Paco were crouched about the lantern. The rays of the uncertain yellow flame made the faces of those below hollow and wolfish.

Lars studied them intently as he listened.

"You're armed now," said Paco in prison French. "Stop being nervous."

"We're not nervous," said a gaunt devil with hypnotic eyes. "We're restless, that's all."

"Play it right," said Paco, "and we'll have this ship in our control before dawn. You sure Flaubert will meet us off the Straits?"

"Certainly," grunted another.

"He'd better have my francs with him," threatened Paco.

"He'll have them. But why worry about francs when we've got a setup like this?" growled a third. "I don't see why we can't pull the trick in Lisbon. . . ."

"And let her get a chance to find out I'm nobody?" scoffed Paco. "No, my friends. I collect my pay for releasing you and then we go partners on what we can get out of this ship."

"She ought to be worth plenty," said the man with hypnotic eyes. "The Norton woman, I mean."

"I'm not worried about what she'll bring in cash," said Paco. "I was hoping I could find a way to play this thing through with her but she'd get next to me and they'd trace me. I won't run that chance."

"What about Lars?" said a burly, shaggy-haired giant who had not spoken before. "Are you sure of him?"

"You know about him," said Paco.

"Sure," said the thin one, "too good for the rest of us. I was hoping we wouldn't have to trust him. Flaubert is as good as Lars Marlin with a sextant. Look, Paco. Have we got all the guns aboard?"

"Lars has a rack full. I sweet-talked Terry into getting them away." Paco laughed as silently as he could. "She thinks he's

70

a pretty desperate character. But he's stuck so close to the bridge we wouldn't chance it before. Johnson is supposed to get the guns and deliver them to Terry as soon as he can. He's got another set of keys."

"Then when do we act?" said the man with the wild stare. "I'm sick of this damned hold."

"I'll give you the signal. We'll be off the Straits soon enough and we can run her somehow until Flaubert boards us."

Lars had drawn his .38. He weighed his chances of getting them all and found his chances very bad. Perhaps he could get one, even two, but by that time the others, guns at their sides, would have fired. If he could get to the bridge before they took his guns and if he could arm the crew . . .

He knew these men. Knew them as the hardest-bitten lot of the Colony. Jean Patou was the fellow with the strange eyes—a jewel thief who had amassed a fortune before he was sent down under. Auberville was the wasted one, a man with two French and four Colony murders to his discredit. The big shaggy man was Tallien, a brooding, vicious devil, who could crack a man's spine with his two hands—and had. The last was obese Renoir, a man of small caste in the Colony but of great importance to France. Renoir had been a politician in his time and his records were many. People wanted to be sure that Renoir's records were never opened.

Four million francs had been a small price for the release of these from French Guiana!

Lars knew that his debt was to Terry Norton. In spite of the pleasure drilling Paco would have given him, he was forced to forgo it. Of the whole company, Lars was the only man who stood a chance of blocking these men. To have asked them to hold up their hands would have been requesting that they shoot instantly.

The hold could not be blocked against exit.

Lars slid back down the incline of boxes. He had to keep his riot guns and after that . . .

Quickly he made his way out of the hold and up the ladder. He strode across the deck to the bridge and mounted swiftly.

Johnson, on watch, gave him a guilty glance as he passed. Lars, with sinking heart, swung into his cabin.

The racks were blank!

He whirled and entered the bridge again. Johnson was crouched back defensively but Lars wasted no talk on him. He went, instead, to the charting table and snatched up a pencil. With a hard, violent hand he flung a black line straight east of their course. He read the compass.

Back on the bridge, he grabbed the wheel from the startled helmsman. Then, in contrast to his stormy mood, he gently passed the spokes through his capable fingers. So gently did the *Valiant* swing that only a slight change in the motion of the waves under her gave a clue to the fact that she had been shifted on her course.

Lars stepped back and shoved the helmsman to his post. "Hold on sixty-one until further orders."

He turned. Johnson, seeing Lars did not blast him, had gained something of courage. "Look here, Captain. I've got orders . . ."

"*You've* got orders," said Lars. "Look here, mister, as long as I can walk I'm master of this vessel. See that he holds that course or you'll answer for it at the first port we touch. Have you got that?"

"Y-Y-Yes."

Lars turned on his heel and clattered down the ladder to the main deck. As he had supposed, Aunt Agatha and Terry, Rosey and Alice, Kenneth and Ralph were all to be found in the salon despite the hour.

Lars entered and slammed the door behind him.

Startled by the noise and then his manner, Terry stared at him.

"Miss Norton," said Lars. "You have had the guns removed from my cabin. You will please tell me immediately where I can find them. I know now why Paco—"

"Captain Lowenskold," said Terry. "It would seem that your tone is rather harsh for a man in such precarious circumstances."

"I am not interested in my circumstances. I am only concerned about yours. Miss Norton, unless I have full command of this situation, you will regret it."

"I do not like your tone," said Terry, standing. "If I saw fit to remove those weapons from your reach, that is what my judgment demanded."

"You mean that is what Paco demanded," said Lars bitterly. "Here and now, Miss Norton, I've got to tell you something which I haven't told you before. I have been thinking of my own—"

"I am afraid I already know what you have to tell me, Captain. His Highness has apologized many times for recommending you but of course he could not have known that your past is not all it is supposed to be. His Highness received a letter which he did not open until we were at sea and then it was too late. He told me over a week ago—"

"He's lying!" cried Lars. "You're being made a fool of! Paco Corvino is no more His Highness than I am the Prince of Wales! He's a murdering devil! He killed—"

"Go on," purred Paco, behind Lars. "Make a fool of yourself, Lars."

Lars whirled to meet Paco's contemptuous smile—and the gun in Paco's hand.

"I told you," said Paco to Terry, "that Lars is sometimes unmanageable. I am sorry that this outbreak had to occur, ladies. It grieves me that it was my word which subjected you to this. If Johnson is at all competent to sail the *Valiant* on into Lisbon, I think we would be safer if we placed poor Lars in a locked cabin and placed a guard over him."

The others were on their feet, staring blankly at this sudden tableau. Rosey gazed with a sigh upon the bravery of the prince.

"Paco," said Lars, carefully. "Tell them what you brought aboard in those coffins."

Paco smiled. "My money, naturally. If Miss Norton would like, I could show her the contents either now or in the morning. I did not think it important."

"Don't be foolish," said Terry. "We trust you, Your Highness."

"Of course," said Aunt Agatha with an indignant sniff.

"Tell them you've got Auberville and Patou and Renoir and Tallien down there. Tell them you're about to seize this ship. Tell them you received four million francs for this deal."

Paco laughed amusedly. He gave Terry a broad, humorous wink. "Of course, Lars. That is just what I have planned. Come now, old fellow, quiet yourself while we place you in safekeeping. This madness will pass, Miss Norton. I am desolated. If I had known—"

Lars made a lunge for Paco's gun but Paco had read the intention in Lars' eyes. Paco leaped agilely back and fired.

Lightning seared through Lars' shoulder. He was turned by the bullet. Falling, he crashed into the bulkhead.

Paco stood with curling smoke about him, still smiling, apologizing to the ladies.

Sailors were coming from the deck. Four men took Lars in custody.

Lars tried to fight them off but they clung hard.

"Miss Norton!" shouted Lars. "You've got to believe me! Paco is going to attack before dawn! For God's sake, arm the crew!"

"Terry," said Paco, as they hustled Lars away, "if I had known this . . ." Paco was very sad.

CHAPTER NINE

To the Attack

THE brig was dimly lit by the blue bulb outside the bars in the corridor. Lars, sitting hunched on the bunk, was still too big for the place, dwarfing it to the size of a hatbox.

Ralph was nervously giving Lars' arm medical attention. Ralph had read a great deal about first aid, but it was fortunate for Lars, just the same, that the bullet had passed straight through the flesh of his muscular shoulder. And Lars was watching impassively while Ralph sweated and felt green when he touched the sticky blood.

"You've got to do it," said Lars.

"I . . . I can't," whispered Ralph, plastering down the adhesive tape. "Sis would murder me!"

"Paco is going to murder all of us. I've told you where you could find your rifles and ammunition and pistols. Why do you think Paco wants those? You're a sensible fellow, Ralph. You know that I couldn't do anything to this whole ship all by myself."

"I don't dare," said Ralph.

"You call that a trial?"

"No, but—"

"All right. It's Paco's word against mine. And it's your life unless you get this straight here and now. I tell you they're going to attack. You won't need any more proof than that."

"No, but—"

"All right. The minute they strike, you be ready. You get those keys and swipe the riot guns up to the bridge. You take my revolver out of Terry's keeping. And then, when they strike, you hot-foot it down here."

"But how'll we get to the bridge?"

"We go forward on this deck to the engine room. We go up through the fidley. You leave that to me. They won't try to hit at the bridge because they don't think anybody there is armed. And another thing. Keep watch by Miss Norton's door. At dawn, tell her that I'm dying. Tell her anything. But get her down here so she'll be on her way when Paco and the rest crack down. Understand?"

"Sure, but—"

"It's your life and Miss Norton's I'm thinking about, Ralph. You need do nothing if Paco fails to take over the ship."

Ralph got up. His eyes were feverishly bright as he began to understand that there might be excitement in the offing. "Maybe . . . maybe I'll do it."

Lars watched him out, heard the door lock. And then, wearily, he lay back upon his bunk.

In spite of the tension within him he knew he must have slept. A far-off shout came to him. He sat up and swung his legs down.

A shot sounded somewhere forward and Lars was on his feet, hands gripping the bars of the door. He shook them.

His every thought was concentrated upon Ralph. If the boy succeeded in getting Terry down here, if he succeeded in bringing the keys, if he had placed the riot guns on the bridge . . .

Lars knew too well what he himself was doing. How easy it would have been to swing in with Paco. But there were other elements involved besides revenge which had chosen his course for him. Terry Norton's safety was now paramount. Since his play last night he had known that he had been fighting to choose between two paths—his own safety and that of Terry Norton. The girl had won. For Lars, now, there would only be French Guiana or Madame Guillotine, no matter if he won against Paco. He saw that clearly. Until midnight of last night, when he had swung that wheel, he had tried to preserve his hard-won freedom. But all question of doing that was gone.

Hurried footsteps were sounding in the passageway. By the blue light, Lars saw Ralph coming. And with him Ralph dragged Terry. She was protesting, glancing back, anxious about the violent sounds which came from the main deck, the repeated shots.

Ralph inserted the keys in the lock, opened the door and slapped a .45 into Lars' big hand.

"What madness is this?" cried Terry. "I thought you said . . . It's a trick! Ralph, you're crazy! Can't you . . ."

"Shut up," said Lars roughly. "Paco is taking over the *Valiant*. We can get to the bridge from the engine room."

Terry stared at him. Shots were more frequent now on deck.

"Are you coming?" demanded Lars.

She did not move and he scooped her up in his arms and bore her swiftly up the passageway. Ralph, panting excitedly, strove to keep up with Lars' long, anxious strides. Terry's negligee floated behind Lars like a ship's wake. The back of the .45 slide was hard and bruising in Terry's side but, staring at Lars' face in wonder, she did not even feel it.

They reached the engine room, skirting the big Diesels and the shining rails, brushing past an astounded engineer, mounting the iron ladders which led upward.

At the top of the last stage, Lars set Terry down. "You'll have to climb. I'll go first."

Lars mounted the precarious rungs up the sheer side. In a moment he reached the open fidley. He stopped there, looking toward the bridge on the same level. Dawn faintly lit the world.

Johnson was leaning over the bridge rail, shouting down at the forward deck. A bullet snapped beside his head and he drew back, almost somersaulting in his rush.

Heavy feet thundered on the bridge ladder. Lars slid out of the hatch and stepped quickly to a position commanding the forward part of the bridge.

Tallien, shaggy hair streaming like black smoke behind him, charged into sight. The light was faint but the range was short. He saw Lars and threw the Mannlicher rifle to his shoulder.

Lars shot from the hip.

Tallien's great bulk stood immobile. He took an uncertain step back. Abruptly the rifle clattered to the deck and Tallien shot out of sight, backwards down the bridge ladder.

Lars raced to the rifle and scooped it up, darting back in time to dodge a random shot from below.

Ralph came up on all fours and Terry stood shivering, pressed against the door to the radio room. It opened against her and the sleepy operator stuck out his head.

"What the hell's the shooting . . . ? Oh, beg pardon, Miss Norton, how—"

Lars was at her side. "Get a radio to Casablanca, French Morocco. Tell them Renoir and Patou are attacking the *Valiant.* Tell them to get a cruiser or anything out here instantly."

"Where are we?"

"About fifty miles straight west of Casablanca." Lars turned to the bridge. "I'll give you the position exactly in a minute."

Terry was swept along by Lars. He thrust her into the protection of the chart room. "Get down out of sight!"

Ralph was digging the riot guns from beneath a transom. A bullet shattered the glass over his head and he ducked. Lars crouched and fired forward at the fo'c's'le head.

"This is going to be hot," said Lars. He looked up as Johnson came in on hands and knees, and grabbed a riot gun from Ralph, shoving it into Johnson's hands. "If you want to live, don't be afraid to use this."

"What's it all about?" quavered Johnson.

Lars had no time to explain, going swiftly in a crouch he got to the wheel. The helmsman was lying on his stomach, afraid to reach up as high as the lowest spoke. Lars took a quick glance at the binnacle. A bullet greeted his rising, shrieking as it struck an inch from his face. But he had what he wanted. The compass still read sixty-one.

Johnson was lying beside him.

"You didn't change the course?"

"I . . . I was scared to. I thought I better put into Casablanca because you threw us off and with all these islands—"

"Good! Ralph! Take this to Sparks!"

Lars handed their position, as swiftly as he could figure it, to Ralph who scuttled away.

Above the short cracks of pistol and rifle below, the whine of a dynamo began to rise. The message was on its way.

The sniper on the fo'c's'le head was getting close, firing at random through the dodger. Splinters plowed up beside Ralph's hand and he quickly stuck his fingers in his mouth to suck the blood from the cuts.

"Won't they attack from the boat deck?" said Johnson.

"I'm going to cover that. You keep these two forward ladders clear."

As Lars crawled past the chart room he saw Terry shivering against the legs of the table. But, no matter how much he wanted to speak to her before the French came, he could not stop.

Lugging a riot gun, he crept toward the boat deck.

He heard Terry's scream, "Look out!"

He spun about. Blond Jean Patou's wild eyes were staring down the sights of a Mann-Scho. Lars fired while still in motion. The two shots roared together. Glass showered down upon Lars. Clumsy, crazy Patou knew little about rifle sights.

Clumsy Jean Patou fell forward on the rifle.

Lars was motionless for an instant. He had hoped it was

Paco. But Paco would hardly take part in such an attack unless it was from the fo'c's'le head.

Shots were coming from that direction now with greater regularity. Lars glanced up at a searchlight platform over the bridge.

Then, using Jean Patou for a barricade, he sent five shots from the riot gun toward the fo'c's'le head. He saw Paco bob back and knew that all five had missed.

But his object was accomplished. Quickly, Lars swarmed up the ladder to the searchlight stage. He threw himself down behind the narrow base. Three swift shots bit steel around him. He reloaded and returned them.

Something changed about the ship and then Lars knew. The engines had stopped. Paco, in the protection of the steel bulkheads forward, also knew it.

Paco's voice was thin but jeering. "Now what are you going to do? We'll starve you out! We'll make you surrender. Don't forget we've got the rest of our pets cooped up and the crew to boot!"

"Ever hear of a radio?" shouted Lars.

An incredulous silence followed this. For a space of minutes no shots were fired, no voice was raised.

And then a wail came from forward. "You wouldn't! You haven't got the nerve to send that radio! You know what they'd do to you!"

"A gunboat's on its way from Casablanca!" shouted Lars. "A French gunboat!"

"Damn you!" screamed Paco. "It's that woman! You fool,

let us have the bridge and we'll get out of here before they come! *They'll get you too!*"

"Sure they will!" cried Lars, jubilant. "Sure they will but it's worth the price. You and I started out from Casablanca. It's fitting that we've come back. But it's not the Penal Colony now. It's the guillotine! The guillotine for the lot of us! If it's the station ship, it'll be Captain Renard. There's no greasing out of this. He knows us. Both of us!"

A bullet shrieked away from the searchlight stanchion. Paco and Renoir and Auberville were firing wildly now. But they knew what had happened to Tallien and Patou and they did not have the courage for another charge.

For two sweating, grimy hours they held the bridge defenders and then, in the east, a smoke plume could be seen. The battle was over.

CHAPTER TEN

The Reckoning

THE station ship stood off a few yards from the *Valiant* and both vessels rolled gently upon the quiet sea. A boatload of French Marines and Captain Renard himself warily approached the yacht.

But they need not have felt concern. Paco and Auberville and Renoir were no longer winning and they could no longer fight. The Marines came up a Jacob's ladder to the deck and stood there in two rows, stiffly in command of the situation.

Captain Renard was small and efficient and dapper. But in spite of his size, his voice could carry a good sea mile. In loud French he bawled, "Do you come out or do we come in?"

Paco came out, head down, shuffling. He appeared punctured. Auberville and Renoir were fatalistic about it. They followed Paco with a truculent stride.

Captain Renard saw Paco but he did not immediately recognize him. Instead he turned his attention on the bridge. Terry Norton was coming down the ladder. Although she was not dressed for such a reception, the gallant captain had no attention to spare for her clothes. He swept off his hat.

"*M'selle!*" said Captain Renard, bowing. "You are Miss Norton. Oh, yes, once I have seen you in Paris! How could I ever forget so exquisite a face. Ah, so sorry you have trouble with these convicts. But, no matter, *I* have arrived. These, of course, *are* the men."

"Yes," said Terry. "This is Paco Corvino."

Paco looked down at the deck.

Members of the ship's company straggled out of the hold and the companionways, ashamed of the part they, unarmed, had been forced to play.

Lars came slowly down from the searchlight platform. His face was bleeding where chips of steel had cut him. He stopped on the bridge to look down. He wanted to watch this for a moment before he became a part of it.

Terry and Captain Renard were still talking. She was trying to tell him what she knew about it.

"You say Paco Corvino?" said Captain Renard. "Wait. I know that name somehow . . . Ah . . ." He faced Paco, roughly squared him around, looking at him as though he inspected some particularly slimy type of spider. "Of course! Paco! But I thought . . . There was a record of your death when you tried to escape. . . . Ah, certainly. You had to lie even about your dying. Miss Norton, I am so sorree, this fellow is the worst blackguard who ever befouled French soil. He is too low to be considered for an instant—except perhaps by the executioner who considers all things for a certain price. I could not express how badly I feel that you have had this trouble from such a worthless, lying miscreant, Miss Norton. I once put it away in the Penal Colony for contraband but it persists in living. Bah, we should squash such things beneath our heel."

He gave Paco a contemptuous thrust and sent him reeling

back into the ranks of Marines. Then he carefully took out a kerchief and as carefully wiped his fingers.

Lars watched the Frenchman and Terry come up toward the bridge. He braced himself. He had seen how Renard had treated Paco and it pleased him. But Lars knew his own turn was coming down. To be humbled before Terry Norton . . .

"If it had not been for a captain we were fortunate enough to procure in Rio," Terry was saying as they came up the ladder, "Paco might have succeeded. But as it was Captain Lowenskold acted so bravely that he kept them at bay. I was very foolish. I would not listen to Captain Lowenskold because Paco—"

"I should like to meet this brave captain."

"He was very anxious to meet you," said Terry. "He sent that radio as fast as Sparks could throw in a switch."

"So?" said Renard. "Then he knew we French were always on the *alerte*! A wise man to send particularly for me!"

Lars was waiting beside the wheel when they reached the top of the ladder. He was watching Renard. Renard could not help but recognize Lars Marlin, the man he had sent up with Paco, now that Paco had been called to Renard's mind. And besides, by this time, all French vessels knew that Lars Marlin, escaped convict, was captaining the *Valiant*. Delal would have traced it by now.

"Captain Renard," said Terry, "may I present Captain Lowenskold?"

Renard's smile suddenly froze on his face. His half-extended hand stayed motionless. Lars read recognition in those eyes.

Renard knew him. Lars wished fervently that it did not have to come before Terry.

Renard scowled a little and withdrew his hand. "You say, Miss Norton, that this man defended you against Paco Corvino?"

"Of course!"

Renard looked at Lars with a studious eye. "Captain *Lowenskold*?" He saw the wounded shoulder and the cut face.

"Yes," said Terry. "It was only his quick thinking which spared us. I doubt any of us would have thought to send for you until it was too late."

"*You* sent for *me*?" said Renard carefully.

Lars neither spoke nor moved.

Terry could feel the tension but she could not understand it.

Renard was trying to think.

A sergeant of marines came to the top of the ladder. "Captain, sir, that jackal Paco Corvino says Lars Marlin is up there and you better bring him down with the others."

"Lars Marlin," said Renard, nodding. He looked around at the shambles of the bridge and looked back at Lars' wounded arm and cut face. Again he looked around him. He could see the dead Tallien's left foot sticking through one ladder. He could see Jean Patou crumpled up in the companionway, blond hair matted with blood.

"Is anything wrong?" said Terry.

Renard shrugged. "Wrong? Wrong? No, it is I who have been wrong. Before when . . . before I thought there might be a doubt, but now I am sure."

"I don't understand," said Terry.

"Sir," said the sergeant, "Paco Corvino keeps telling me that Lars Marlin is up there. I remember he was sent up with Paco."

"Your memory does you credit, Sergeant," said Renard. "Go back and tell that ugly louse, Paco Corvino, to be still. Miss Norton, I am so sorry I have troubled you about this, so glad to have been of help."

He suddenly extended his hand to Lars. "I am so glad to have met such a brave man, Captain . . . *Lowenskold*."

Lars took the hand, too stunned to say a word.

"But what is this about another one being up here?" said Terry as Renard moved off.

Captain Renard smiled and shrugged. "He is talking about another convict named Marlin. And anybody with half an eye"—and here he turned dead Jean Patou over with his foot—"could see that *there* lies Marlin, dead as an anchovy."

Captain Renard, very pleased with himself and the world, trotted jauntily down the bridge ladder. He stopped and roared commands at his men, and the sergeant, kicking Paco along before him, cursed Paco all the way down into the motorboat.

Lars Lowenskold leaned weakly against the binnacle, listening to the departing engine.

Quickly and solicitously, Terry put her small hand on his arm.

Story Preview

Story Preview

NOW that you've just ventured through one of the captivating tales in the Stories from the Golden Age collection by L. Ron Hubbard, turn the page and enjoy a preview of *Loot of the Shanung*. Join Jimmy Vance, an ace reporter who's hired by the beautiful Virginia Rockham to find her missing father, billionaire oil magnate George Harley Rockham, only to become the target himself of several especially vicious thugs.

Loot of the Shanung

T HE press releases flowed across the desk in a miniature Yangtze at flood time. The office of the *Oriental Press* throbbed with effort and excitement.

Jimmy Vance, both hands full and a pencil between his teeth, stared up at the copy boy. "Here y'are. Tell them to run this on the first page. I'll hand the fills over in a few minutes. About his life and all."

"A lady to see you, Jimmy," said the copy boy.

"The devil with that. Where'd I put that *Who's Who?*"

The *Who's Who* came to light when it was going down for the third time in the tan copy paper. Jimmy flipped it open, swept his very blond hair out of his eyes, and ran his finger down the column.

"George Harley Rockham," said the *Who's Who.* "Born 1890 in Chicago, Ill. Appointed to Russian Wheat Commission, 1919. Served as Secretary of Interior, 1924–6. Held oil leases in Regular Oil Company. Developed vast holdings in South America. Created an oil monopoly in China, 1928. Known best through his hobby of travel. Married Virginia Courtney in 1908. His daughter, Miss Virginia Rockham, has long been known to Long Island Society. . . ."

"Huh," said Jimmy, "that's plenty. Plenty." He grabbed at his battered typewriter, inserted half a dozen sheets after the custom of copywriters and began to hammer the keys in an industrious hunt-and-punch system.

The copy boy, bucktoothed and mostly grin, was at his elbow again. "Jimmy. That dame says she won't wait. You got to see her. Here's the card."

"Busy," said Jimmy, continuing to write.

"She's a swell looker," informed the copy boy. "Real class."

"Beat it," said Jimmy, scowling at the *Who's Who*.

His story grew out of the roller:

Shanghai, China, May 14, *Oriental Press*. As the fate of George Harley Rockham, the great oil magnate, tonight remained shrouded with mystery, his many friends over the world watched anxiously for the first news.

Jimmy scratched his head, scowled at the sheet and then wrote:

It is debated that he still lives. The coastal steamer *Shanung* has not appeared in Hong Kong, and while there are no storms recorded north of that city, it is thought that the *Shanung* might have foundered, run aground or met any other perils of the sea.

Rumor is current that the *Shanung* was captured by the notorious pirates who range along Bias Bay, a few miles north of Hong Kong. This is only one of many conjectures that . . .

The copy boy was there again, still grinning. "That dame gave me a five-spot to see you, Jimmy. Y'can't let me down now. I need five Mex and if you don't see her I'll have to give it back."

"Scram," said Jimmy, pondering anew. He was about to consult the *Who's Who* for further rumors, conjectures and so on when he became aware of a pair of hands on the railing before his desk.

He stopped, looking absently at the fingers. They were nice hands. White and graceful, with long, naturally polished nails. A diamond ring glittered, but it wasn't on the engagement finger.

Jimmy was suddenly interested. He looked up the arms and discovered a Cossack jacket with silver cartridge cases. He looked at the high Russian collar and then saw the face.

The face, decided Jimmy, was very pleasing. The girl's eyes were dark, rather wistful and sad. Her cheekbones were high, giving an air of severity to the features. But the fullness of the good-natured mouth belied that.

"You're Jimmy Vance?" said the girl, very quietly.

"Yes," said Jimmy and then instantly recovered himself. "If you're looking for the society editor, he's first corridor to your right." He turned back to his work, not meaning to be rude, but aware of the necessity of stopping the study of the girl.

He was about to write another paragraph on the story when he saw the card the boy had laid beside his typewriter. The card was simply engraved. It said, "Virginia Rockham."

Jimmy's eyes flashed up. It was one of the few times in Jimmy's headlong career that he registered surprise. He jumped to his feet and swung the gate back.

"Good golly, Miss Rockham. I'm sorry as the devil. I thought you must be one of these Ruskies, the way you're dressed. I didn't have any idea . . . Here, have a chair. Now listen, Miss Rockham, I've got to have some dope here before I can go on."

She was mildly surprised at his manner. Jimmy usually gave the impression of a meteor in full flight. He was not so very tall and he seemed utterly without color. His eyes were big and swift and frank. He had the air of hurrying even when sitting still. Restlessly, he offered her a cigarette and then lit one for himself when she refused.

"Dope, Miss Rockham. The presses are grinding, the boys are waiting on the streets. The international cables are holding down their keys, waiting for this stuff. I've heard opinions, I've heard theories, and now, by golly, I want to hear some facts."

"I . . . I don't know any more than you do, Mr. Vance."

"The hell you don't!" Jimmy was plainly aghast. "Well . . . well . . . think of something, anything. I've written columns on it already and I've had to make up each and every word. Good God, Miss Rockham, a billionaire doesn't disappear like that. Even out here in China. He has to be *someplace*. Even a Chinese pirate would know how much he was worth in ransom. Think, girl!"

She was studying Jimmy, listening to his voice rather than his words. Her dark eyes were suddenly alight. She sat forward.

"You're *the* Jimmy Vance, aren't you?" she said.

He was thrown into no little confusion, but he recovered quickly. "What do you mean by that?"

"You're the man who makes news news, aren't you? The

star reporter of the *Oriental Press*, the bearder of warlords and the formulator of international opinions."

Jimmy gaped at her. "Gee whiz, Miss Rockham . . . I . . . Somebody has been feeding you a line. Look here, Miss Rockham, I got to have something for the presses, the cables. I got to have *fact* not fancy. What happened to your father?"

"He was on the SS *Shanung*. The *Shanung* isn't reported. That's all I know."

"But look here. I mean what's the well-known lowdown? What's he tied up with? Who's trying to get him? What's hanging over his head?"

"I thought . . . thought you'd know something about it," she replied.

"Me? Why should I know anything? I'm just a dumb reporter, Miss Rockham. I admit I've had a few breaks, but does that make a clairvoyant out of me? Hell, no. I mean to say, I don't know anything and I'm writing guesses."

"This is big news, isn't it?"

"Big news? Gee whiz, Miss Rockham, I'll say it is. Might as well have the president of the United States disappear as George Harley Rockham. He's got China oil in his palm. He owns more men and more companies than a nation. What made him disappear?"

"He went down to Hong Kong to look over some interests there. That's all I know."

Jimmy leaned tensely over his typewriter. "Where was he before that?"

"Chinwangtao."

"Up next to Manchukuo, right? What's he own in Manchukuo?"

"I'm not certain."

Jimmy smiled a swift smile. "Then he *does* own something. Why did—?"

"Wait, Mr. Vance. We're wasting time here. I came up for just one reason. I came here to see Jimmy Vance to offer him a job. I've been told and I know for myself that if anyone can find George Harley Rockham and do the job quickly, it would be Jimmy Vance. Speed is your name."

"Why speed?"

The girl's voice was low and earnest, "Because Rockham isn't as steady as a rock the way the advertisements read. He holds his industrial empire together with one finger, but when that finger slips . . ." She reached into her handbag and threw a cable report of stocks on Wall Street on Jimmy's typewriter keys.

"See those stocks?" she said, tensely. "They've lost points! And Rockham isn't here. Because he's gone, they're selling him out. If we don't find him in four days and tell the world he's safe, George Harley Rockham will be on the relief rolls. That's not for publication, Mr. Vance. That's truth. We've *got* to find him!"

To find out more about *Loot of the Shanung* and how you can obtain your copy, go to www.goldenagestories.com.

Glossary

Glossary

STORIES FROM THE GOLDEN AGE *reflect the words and expressions used in the 1930s and 1940s, adding unique flavor and authenticity to the tales. While a character's speech may often reflect regional origins, it also can convey attitudes common in the day. So that readers can better grasp such cultural and historical terms, uncommon words or expressions of the era, the following glossary has been provided.*

---

afterdeck: the part of the ship's deck between the midships section and the stern.

Alphonse XIII: (1886–1941) king of Spain from 1886–1931.

anchorage: that portion of a harbor, or area outside a harbor, suitable for anchoring, or in which ships are permitted to anchor.

Aragon: a region and former kingdom of northeast Spain.

bales: large bundles or packages prepared for shipping, storage, etc.

bandolier: a broad belt worn over the shoulder by soldiers and having a number of small loops or pockets for holding cartridges.

bearder: one who boldly confronts or challenges (someone formidable).

before the mast: the forward part of the ship, where common sailors have their quarters.

bells: the strokes on a ship's bell, every half-hour, to mark the passage of time.

benj: (Persian) marijuana; also called *bhang;* in one of the stories of *The Arabian Nights,* it is used to drug a wine, producing a deathlike sleep.

Bias Bay: body of water off the coast of China, fifty miles northeast of Hong Kong, and notorious as a base of operations for Chinese pirates.

binnacle: a built-in housing for a ship's compass.

blackguard: a man who behaves in a dishonorable or contemptible way.

book: (cards) in bridge, the number of tricks (usually six) that a side must win before it can score by winning subsequent tricks.

bridge wing: a narrow walkway extending outward from both sides of a pilothouse to the full width of a ship.

Burma: country in southeast Asia on the Bay of Bengal now known as Myanmar.

Canary Islands: a group of islands off the northwestern coast of Africa belonging to Spain.

Cape Frio: coastal city in Brazil located in the state of Rio de Janeiro.

Carioca Range: a small coastal mountain range running east to west through the city of Rio de Janeiro.

Casablanca: a seaport on the Atlantic coast of Morocco.

Cayenne: a seaport and the capital of French Guiana. It was the location of a French penal settlement from 1854 to 1938 and was known as *la guillotine sèche* or *the dry guillotine.* Devil's Island, another French penal colony at that time, was located nearby.

cayman: a reptile related to the alligator but smaller and slimmer and with a proportionally longer tail. Native to tropical America.

Chinwangtao: port city of northwest China on the Bo Hai Sea, an inlet of the Yellow Sea, 186 miles (300 km) east of Beijing. It was formerly a treaty port where foreign trade was allowed.

clipper: a sailing ship built and rigged for speed, especially a type of three-masted ship. Used in trade winds in which speed was more important than cargo capacity.

coasting: sailing along or near a coast, or running between ports along a coast. A coasting vessel is employed in trade by water between neighboring ports of the same country, as distinguished from foreign trade or trade involving long voyages.

Coast Pilot: official publication giving descriptions of particular sections of a coast and usually sailing directions for coastal navigation.

Cossack jacket: *cherkeska;* a military coatlike garment with silver cartridges lined across the chest. The cartridges are a reminder of the times when the Cossacks were armed with muzzle-loading guns. At that time, each cartridge contained enough gunpowder for one shot. When breech-loading weapons came into use, the holders were retained as part of the costume.

de Milo: Venus de Milo; famous Greek sculpture of Venus, the goddess of love and beauty.

Devil's Island: an island in the Caribbean Sea off French Guiana and location of a notorious French penal colony, opened in 1854 and closed in 1946. Used by France, its inmates were everything from political prisoners to the most hardened of thieves and murderers. Conditions were harsh and many prisoners sent there were never seen again. Few convicts ever managed to escape.

dodger: a canvas or wood screen to provide protection from ocean spray on a ship.

drill: a strong, twilled cotton fabric.

dynamo: a machine by which mechanical energy is changed into electrical energy; a generator.

ennui: a feeling of utter weariness and discontent resulting from a lack of interest; boredom.

fidley: an area above ship boilers designed for the intake of fresh air. Fidley grates prevent people or objects from falling into the boiler room.

five-spot: a five-dollar bill.

flotsam: vagrant, usually destitute people.

fo'c's'le head: forecastle head; the part of the upper deck of a ship at the front. The forecastle is the front of a ship, from the name of the raised castlelike deck on some early sailing vessels, built to overlook and control the enemy's deck.

French Guiana: a French colony of northeast South America on the Atlantic Ocean, established in the nineteenth century and known for its penal colonies (now closed). Cayenne is the capital and the largest city.

gangway: a narrow, movable platform or ramp forming a bridge by which to board or leave a ship.

Gávea: peak in Rio de Janeiro located by the sea between two beaches and rising 2,762 feet above sea level.

G-men: government men; agents of the Federal Bureau of Investigation.

Grand Banks: shallow section of the Atlantic Ocean off southeastern Canada that is an important fishing region. The mixing of cold and warm water currents and the relative shallowness of the water has made this one of the richest international fishing grounds in the world.

gumshoes: sneakers or rubber overshoes.

hawser: a thick rope or cable for mooring or towing a ship.

hooker: an older vessel, usually a cargo boat.

Hunchback: peak in Rio de Janeiro, on top of which stands the famous statue of Jesus Christ that watches over the city.

Indochina: the former French colonial empire in southeast Asia, including much of the eastern part of the Indochinese peninsula (now Vietnam, Laos and Cambodia). French influence extended from roughly 1862 through 1954.

Jacob's ladder: a hanging ladder having ropes or chains supporting wooden or metal rungs or steps.

knot: a unit of speed, equal to one nautical mile, or about 1.15 miles, per hour.

lighters: large open flat-bottomed barges, used in loading and unloading ships offshore or in transporting goods for short distances in shallow waters.

Manchukuo: a former state of eastern Asia in Manchuria and eastern Inner Mongolia. In 1932 it was established as a puppet state (a country that is nominally independent, but in reality is under the control of another power) after the Japanese invaded Manchuria in 1931. It was returned to the Chinese government in 1945.

Mannlicher: a type of rifle equipped with a manually operated sliding bolt for loading cartridges for firing, as opposed to the more common rotating bolt of other rifles. Mannlicher rifles were considered reasonably strong and accurate.

Mann-Scho: Mannlicher-Schoenauer; a rifle introduced in 1903 that proved very popular with big-game hunters worldwide. Its main feature was the use of a magazine that automatically rotated the rounds into the feeding position while the gun was being fired.

Mex: Mexican peso; in 1732 it was introduced as a trade coin with China and was so popular that China became one of its principal consumers. Mexico minted and exported pesos to China until 1949. It was issued as both coins and paper money.

milréis: (Portuguese) a former Brazilian monetary unit.

Morocco: a country of northwest Africa on the Mediterranean Sea and the Atlantic Ocean. The French established a protectorate over most of the region in 1912, and in 1956 Morocco achieved independence as a kingdom.

Mt. Cépéron: a mountain in Cayenne, a seaport and the capital of French Guiana. On this mount stands Fort St.

Michel, the marine barracks, the signal station and the lighthouse.

peerages: books listing the titles of nobility in various countries, the members of nobility and information about their families.

Pernambuco: state in northeastern Brazil.

Pico: Pico de Papagaio (Parrot's Peak), a mountain peak located at the mouth of the Guanabara Bay in Rio de Janeiro, Brazil. The bay is flanked by Pico de Papagaio on one side and by Pão de Açúcar (Sugar Loaf) on the other.

pip: something extraordinary of its kind.

put in or **put into:** to enter a port or harbor, especially for shelter, repairs or provisions.

queer: to ruin or thwart.

salade: a light, late medieval helmet with a brim flaring in the back to protect the neck, sometimes fitted with a visor.

Scheherazade: the female narrator of *The Arabian Nights,* who during one thousand and one adventurous nights saved her life by entertaining her husband, the king, with stories.

Schoenauer: Mannlicher-Schoenauer; a rifle introduced in 1903 that proved very popular with big-game hunters worldwide. Its main feature was the use of a magazine that automatically rotated the rounds into the feeding position while the gun was being fired.

schooner: a fast sailing ship with at least two masts and with sails set lengthwise.

screw: a ship's propeller.

set: in the card game of bridge, to defeat an opponent.

Shanghai: city of eastern China at the mouth of the Yangtze River, and the largest city in the country. Shanghai was opened to foreign trade by treaty in 1842 and quickly prospered. France, Great Britain and the United States all held large concessions (rights to use land granted by a government) in the city until the early twentieth century.

"sleeping giant": the northeast face of the peak Gávea in Rio de Janeiro that has a carving of an ancient face resembling that of the Sphinx in Egypt.

Sparks: radioman; traditionally nicknamed *Sparks* or *Sparky,* stemming from the early use of transmitters that produced sparks to radiate energy, the means by which radio signals were transmitted.

SS: steamship.

stanchion: an upright bar, post or frame forming a support or barrier.

Sugar Loaf: Pão de Açúcar (Sugar Loaf), a mountain peak located at the mouth of the Guanabara Bay in Rio de Janeiro, Brazil. Its name is said to refer to its resemblance to the traditional shape of a concentrated refined loaf of sugar. The bay is flanked by Pico de Papagaio (Parrot's Peak) on one side and by Pão de Açúcar (Sugar Loaf) on the other.

ticket: a certifying document, especially a captain's or pilot's license.

transom: transom seat; a kind of bench seat, usually with a locker or drawers underneath.

trick: 1. (cards) in bridge, four cards played in sequence, one by each player at the table in a clockwise rotation. The high card is the winner. 2. a period or turn of duty, as at the helm of a ship.

tricolor: the French national flag, consisting of three equal vertical bands of blue, white and red.

Tropic of Capricorn: southern tropic; one of the five major parallels of latitude, it lies approximately 23½ degrees south of the equator. It marks the most southerly latitude at which the sun can appear directly overhead.

twenty-five-twenty: .25-20; a rifle cartridge approximately .25 inch in diameter, originally having a powder charge of 20 grains, which is the source of its name. This size rifle was used for hunting small game.

weigh anchor: take up the anchor when ready to sail. Also used figuratively.

wing: bridge wing; a narrow walkway extending outward from both sides of a pilothouse to the full width of a ship.

L. Ron Hubbard
in the Golden Age
of Pulp Fiction

*In writing an adventure story
a writer has to know that he is adventuring
for a lot of people who cannot.
The writer has to take them here and there
about the globe and show them
excitement and love and realism.
As long as that writer is living the part of an
adventurer when he is hammering
the keys, he is succeeding with his story.*

*Adventuring is a state of mind.
If you adventure through life, you have a
good chance to be a success on paper.*

*Adventure doesn't mean globe-trotting,
exactly, and it doesn't mean great deeds.
Adventuring is like art.
You have to live it to make it real.*

—L. RON HUBBARD

L. Ron Hubbard
and American
Pulp Fiction

B ORN March 13, 1911, L. Ron Hubbard lived a life at least as expansive as the stories with which he enthralled a hundred million readers through a fifty-year career.

Originally hailing from Tilden, Nebraska, he spent his formative years in a classically rugged Montana, replete with the cowpunchers, lawmen and desperadoes who would later people his Wild West adventures. And lest anyone imagine those adventures were drawn from vicarious experience, he was not only breaking broncs at a tender age, he was also among the few whites ever admitted into Blackfoot society as a bona fide blood brother. While if only to round out an otherwise rough and tumble youth, his mother was that rarity of her time—a thoroughly educated woman—who introduced her son to the classics of Occidental literature even before his seventh birthday.

But as any dedicated L. Ron Hubbard reader will attest, his world extended far beyond Montana. In point of fact, and as the son of a United States naval officer, by the age of eighteen he had traveled over a quarter of a million miles. Included therein were three Pacific crossings to a then still mysterious Asia, where he ran with the likes of Her British Majesty's agent-in-place

L. Ron Hubbard, left, at Congressional Airport, Washington, DC, 1931, with members of George Washington University flying club.

for North China, and the last in the line of Royal Magicians from the court of Kublai Khan. For the record, L. Ron Hubbard was also among the first Westerners to gain admittance to forbidden Tibetan monasteries below Manchuria, and his photographs of China's Great Wall long graced American geography texts.

Upon his return to the United States and a hasty completion of his interrupted high school education, the young Ron Hubbard entered George Washington University. There, as fans of his aerial adventures may have heard, he earned his wings as a pioneering barnstormer at the dawn of American aviation. He also earned a place in free-flight record books for the longest sustained flight above Chicago. Moreover, as a roving reporter for *Sportsman Pilot* (featuring his first professionally penned articles), he further helped inspire a generation of pilots who would take America to world airpower.

Immediately beyond his sophomore year, Ron embarked on the first of his famed ethnological expeditions, initially to then untrammeled Caribbean shores (descriptions of which would later fill a whole series of West Indies mystery-thrillers). That the Puerto Rican interior would also figure into the future of Ron Hubbard stories was likewise no accident. For in addition to cultural studies of the island, a 1932–33

LRH expedition is rightly remembered as conducting the first complete mineralogical survey of a Puerto Rico under United States jurisdiction.

There was many another adventure along this vein: As a lifetime member of the famed Explorers Club, L. Ron Hubbard charted North Pacific waters with the first shipboard radio direction finder, and so pioneered a long-range navigation system universally employed until the late twentieth century. While not to put too fine an edge on it, he also held a rare Master Mariner's license to pilot any vessel, of any tonnage in any ocean.

Yet lest we stray too far afield, there is an LRH note at this juncture in his saga, and it reads in part:

"I started out writing for the pulps, writing the best I knew, writing for every mag on the stands, slanting as well as I could."

To which one might add: His earliest submissions date from the summer of 1934, and included tales drawn from true-to-life Asian adventures, with characters roughly modeled on British/American intelligence operatives he had known in Shanghai. His early Westerns were similarly peppered with details drawn from personal experience. Although therein lay a first hard lesson from the often cruel world of the pulps. His first Westerns were soundly rejected as lacking the authenticity of a Max Brand yarn

Capt. L. Ron Hubbard in Ketchikan, Alaska, 1940, on his Alaskan Radio Experimental Expedition, the first of three voyages conducted under the Explorers Club flag.

117

(a particularly frustrating comment given L. Ron Hubbard's Westerns came straight from his Montana homeland, while Max Brand was a mediocre New York poet named Frederick Schiller Faust, who turned out implausible six-shooter tales from the terrace of an Italian villa).

Nevertheless, and needless to say, L. Ron Hubbard persevered and soon earned a reputation as among the most publishable names in pulp fiction, with a ninety percent placement rate of first-draft manuscripts. He was also among the most prolific, averaging between seventy and a hundred thousand words a month. Hence the rumors that L. Ron Hubbard had redesigned a typewriter for faster keyboard action and pounded out manuscripts on a continuous roll of butcher paper to save the precious seconds it took to insert a single sheet of paper into manual typewriters of the day.

That all L. Ron Hubbard stories did not run beneath said byline is yet another aspect of pulp fiction lore. That is, as publishers periodically rejected manuscripts from top-drawer authors if only to avoid paying top dollar, L. Ron Hubbard and company just as frequently replied with submissions under various pseudonyms. In Ron's case, the

A MAN OF MANY NAMES

Between 1934 and 1950, L. Ron Hubbard authored more than fifteen million words of fiction in more than two hundred classic publications. To supply his fans and editors with stories across an array of genres and pulp titles, he adopted fifteen pseudonyms in addition to his already renowned L. Ron Hubbard byline.

Winchester Remington Colt
Lt. Jonathan Daly
Capt. Charles Gordon
Capt. L. Ron Hubbard
Bernard Hubbel
Michael Keith
Rene Lafayette
Legionnaire 148
Legionnaire 14830
Ken Martin
Scott Morgan
Lt. Scott Morgan
Kurt von Rachen
Barry Randolph
Capt. Humbert Reynolds

list included: Rene Lafayette, Captain Charles Gordon, Lt. Scott Morgan and the notorious Kurt von Rachen—supposedly on the lam for a murder rap, while hammering out two-fisted prose in Argentina. The point: While L. Ron Hubbard as Ken Martin spun stories of Southeast Asian intrigue, LRH as Barry Randolph authored tales of

romance on the Western range—which, stretching between a dozen genres is how he came to stand among the two hundred elite authors providing close to a million tales through the glory days of American Pulp Fiction.

L. Ron Hubbard, circa 1930, at the outset of a literary career that would finally span half a century.

In evidence of exactly that, by 1936 L. Ron Hubbard was literally leading pulp fiction's elite as president of New York's American Fiction Guild. Members included a veritable pulp hall of fame: Lester "Doc Savage" Dent, Walter "The Shadow" Gibson, and the legendary Dashiell Hammett—to cite but a few.

Also in evidence of just where L. Ron Hubbard stood within his first two years on the American pulp circuit: By the spring of 1937, he was ensconced in Hollywood, adopting a Caribbean thriller for Columbia Pictures, remembered today as *The Secret of Treasure Island.* Comprising fifteen thirty-minute episodes, the L. Ron Hubbard screenplay led to the most profitable matinée serial in Hollywood history. In accord with Hollywood culture, he was thereafter continually called upon

The 1937 Secret of Treasure Island, *a fifteen-episode serial adapted for the screen by L. Ron Hubbard from his novel,* Murder at Pirate Castle.

to rewrite/doctor scripts—most famously for long-time friend and fellow adventurer Clark Gable.

In the interim—and herein lies another distinctive chapter of the L. Ron Hubbard story—he continually worked to open Pulp Kingdom gates to up-and-coming authors. Or, for that matter, anyone who wished to write. It was a fairly unconventional stance, as markets were already thin and competition razor sharp. But the fact remains, it was an L. Ron Hubbard hallmark that he vehemently lobbied on behalf of young authors—regularly supplying instructional articles to trade journals, guest-lecturing to short story classes at George Washington University and Harvard, and even founding his own creative writing competition. It was established in 1940, dubbed the Golden Pen, and guaranteed winners both New York representation and publication in *Argosy*.

But it was John W. Campbell Jr.'s *Astounding Science Fiction* that finally proved the most memorable LRH vehicle. While every fan of L. Ron Hubbard's galactic epics undoubtedly knows the story, it nonetheless bears repeating: By late 1938, the pulp publishing magnate of Street & Smith was determined to revamp *Astounding Science Fiction* for broader readership. In particular, senior editorial director F. Orlin Tremaine called for stories with a stronger *human element*. When acting editor John W. Campbell balked, preferring his spaceship-driven tales, Tremaine enlisted Hubbard. Hubbard, in turn, replied with the genre's first truly *character-driven* works, wherein heroes are pitted not against bug-eyed monsters but the mystery and majesty of deep space itself—and thus was launched the Golden Age of Science Fiction.

The names alone are enough to quicken the pulse of any science fiction aficionado, including LRH friend and protégé, Robert Heinlein, Isaac Asimov, A. E. van Vogt and Ray Bradbury. Moreover, when coupled with LRH stories of fantasy, we further come to what's rightly been described as the foundation of every modern tale of horror: L. Ron Hubbard's immortal *Fear.* It was rightly proclaimed by Stephen King as one of the very few works to genuinely warrant that overworked term "classic"—as in: *"This is a classic tale of creeping, surreal menace and horror. . . . This is one of the really, really good ones."*

To accommodate the greater body of L. Ron Hubbard fantasies, Street & Smith inaugurated *Unknown*—a classic pulp if there ever was one, and wherein readers were soon thrilling to the likes of *Typewriter in the Sky* and *Slaves of Sleep* of which Frederik Pohl would declare: *"There are bits and pieces from Ron's work that became part of the language in ways that very few other writers managed."*

L. Ron Hubbard, 1948, among fellow science fiction luminaries at the World Science Fiction Convention in Toronto.

And, indeed, at J. W. Campbell Jr.'s insistence, Ron was regularly drawing on themes from the Arabian Nights and so introducing readers to a world of genies, jinn, Aladdin and Sinbad—all of which, of course, continue to float through cultural mythology to this day.

At least as influential in terms of post-apocalypse stories was L. Ron Hubbard's 1940 *Final Blackout*. Generally acclaimed as the finest anti-war novel of the decade and among the ten best works of the genre ever authored—here, too, was a tale that would live on in ways few other writers imagined.

Portland, Oregon, 1943; L. Ron Hubbard, captain of the US Navy subchaser PC 815.

Hence, the later Robert Heinlein verdict: "Final Blackout *is as perfect a piece of science fiction as has ever been written.*"

Like many another who both lived and wrote American pulp adventure, the war proved a tragic end to Ron's sojourn in the pulps. He served with distinction in four theaters and was highly decorated for commanding corvettes in the North Pacific. He was also grievously wounded in combat, lost many a close friend and colleague and thus resolved to say farewell to pulp fiction and devote himself to what it had supported these many years—namely, his serious research.

But in no way was the LRH literary saga at an end, for as he wrote some thirty years later, in 1980:

"Recently there came a period when I had little to do. This was novel in a life so crammed with busy years, and I decided to amuse myself by writing a novel that was pure science fiction."

That work was *Battlefield Earth: A Saga of the Year 3000*. It was an immediate *New York Times* bestseller and, in fact, the first international science fiction blockbuster in decades. It was not, however, L. Ron Hubbard's magnum opus, as that distinction is generally reserved for his next and final work: The 1.2 million word *Mission Earth*.

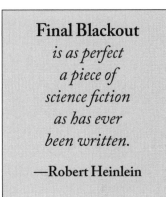

Final Blackout
is as perfect
a piece of
science fiction
as has ever
been written.

—Robert Heinlein

How he managed those 1.2 million words in just over twelve months is yet another piece of the L. Ron Hubbard legend. But the fact remains, he did indeed author a ten-volume *dekalogy* that lives in publishing history for the fact that each and every volume of the series was also a *New York Times* bestseller.

Moreover, as subsequent generations discovered L. Ron Hubbard through republished works and novelizations of his screenplays, the mere fact of his name on a cover signaled an international bestseller. . . . Until, to date, sales of his works exceed hundreds of millions, and he otherwise remains among the most enduring and widely read authors in literary history. Although as a final word on the tales of L. Ron Hubbard, perhaps it's enough to simply reiterate what editors told readers in the glory days of American Pulp Fiction:

He writes the way he does, brothers, because he's been there, seen it and done it!

THE STORIES FROM THE GOLDEN AGE

Your ticket to adventure starts here with the Stories from
the Golden Age collection by master storyteller L. Ron Hubbard.
These gripping tales are set in a kaleidoscope of exotic locales and brim
with fascinating characters, including some of the
most vile villains, dangerous dames and brazen heroes
you'll ever get to meet.

The entire collection of over one hundred and fifty stories is being
released in a series of eighty books and audiobooks.
For an up-to-date listing of available titles,
go to www.goldenagestories.com.

AIR ADVENTURE

Arctic Wings
The Battling Pilot
Boomerang Bomber
The Crate Killer
The Dive Bomber
Forbidden Gold
Hurtling Wings
The Lieutenant Takes the Sky

Man-Killers of the Air
On Blazing Wings
Red Death Over China
Sabotage in the Sky
Sky Birds Dare!
The Sky-Crasher
Trouble on His Wings
Wings Over Ethiopia

FAR-FLUNG ADVENTURE

SEA ADVENTURE

TALES FROM THE ORIENT

The Devil—With Wings   *Pearl Pirate*
The Falcon Killer   *The Red Dragon*
Five Mex for a Million   *Spy Killer*
Golden Hell   *Tah*
The Green God   *The Trail of the Red Diamonds*
Hurricane's Roar   *Wind-Gone-Mad*
Inky Odds   *Yellow Loot*
Orders Is Orders

MYSTERY

The Blow Torch Murder   *The Grease Spot*
Brass Keys to Murder   *Killer Ape*
Calling Squad Cars!   *Killer's Law*
The Carnival of Death   *The Mad Dog Murder*
The Chee-Chalker   *Mouthpiece*
Dead Men Kill   *Murder Afloat*
The Death Flyer   *The Slickers*
Flame City   *They Killed Him Dead*

127

FANTASY

SCIENCE FICTION

WESTERN

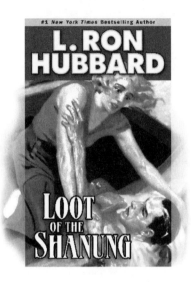